"Come over here, Liz'beth."

Logan's voice was seductively low, and Elizabeth fought down a flutter of desire. "Madman!" she uttered weakly, dragging her eyes from where he lay sprawled on the bed.

"There was a time you would have come freely," he murmured.

Elizabeth stiffened. "Haven't you noticed, Logan? I'm a far cry from that girl you used to know."

He swung his legs off the bed and lazily got to his feet. "I couldn't help but notice," he drawled, closing the space between them. Then his arms were cradling her gently, his lips communicating his hunger.

Senses swimming, her world shifting, Elizabeth managed to gasp, "Goodness, Logan!"

Logan smiled and swept her off her feet. "Goodness has nothing to do with it...."

THE AUTHOR

Gloria Douglas, one of Harlequin's Canadian authors, wrote three novels as "practice" before submitting *Winning Hearts* to Temptation. The moral, she says, is that dreams do come true...but not without a lot of hard work.

Gloria divides her time between writing and making a home for her husband and son in St. Catharines, Ontario.

Winning Hearts

GLORIA DOUGLAS

Harlequin Books

TORONTO • NEW YORK • LONDON
AMSTERDAM • PARIS • SYDNEY • HAMBURG
STOCKHOLM • ATHENS • TOKYO • MILAN

Published December 1985

ISBN 0-373-25188-2

Printed in Canada

1

LOOKING DOWN at the light-spangled backdrop had been a mistake. Elizabeth gripped the railing with white-knuckled tenacity as a wave of vertigo assailed her and blinked thick lashes to counteract the dizzying effects. Carefully she placed her back to the balustrade, letting go of the handrail only momentarily to do so.

"Luke..." she called out in a tiny voice, lifting her ashen face to look up at the photographer perched so precariously on a small ledge above her. "Couldn't this session just as easily be faked? I mean...why couldn't we just use the studio...and then superimpose my image on top of all that," she said, jerking her head backward, not daring to look. A gust of wind caught the long, burnished fullness of her hair, whipping it into photogenic disarray under the arc of lights.

Braced behind the tripod, Luke put his eye to the lens of his new Nikon FA, which he still considered a technological wonder. In a few months he would act blasé about it, but he was crooning now as he brought Elizabeth into focus with the entire city spread out below her. "Ahh," he said, "my little microcomputer friend is assessing and comparing you with the information in its memory bank. And that's based on some hundred thousand photographs that have been analyzed from every technical and aesthetic standpoint. And you know what? It loves you the best, Liz."

Elizabeth lifted her eyes heavenward. "Charmed, I'm sure. But you didn't answer my question. Did you know that the

CN Tower is twice—*twice*—the height of the Eiffel Tower? That it's the tallest free-standing structure in the world?"

"Torontonians try not to brag about that, love. More lighting on her face, Lenny," Luke said to his assistant. "We're advertising cosmetics, not that gossamer creation she's wearing. It's important but incidental to the cause. Now, dear, to answer your question—realism is the key word. Haven't you been hanging around me long enough to know that? Look at that hair—that glorious windblown hair—I rest my case!"

"You've heard of studio fans?" Elizabeth questioned, determined to make her point, as well.

"Yes, and I've also heard you're purported to be Canada's top model. Listen to your favorite photographer, hon. As usual, he knows what's best for you."

Luke Corey had been commissioned by prestigious Rawley Cosmetics to photograph Elizabeth almost exclusively when she became the "Rawley Girl" on their television commercials. Taking stills of her face and figure was Luke's job, and she had to admit he was a painstaking master at it, putting her special image on billboards and magazines countrywide. No shot was too adventurous, no interesting location too far away. As a result, she had been traveling with Luke and his various assistants for the past several weeks, creating a backlog of photographs to tide them over the summer months ahead so that Elizabeth could take a much-needed rest. She had been working practically nonstop for the past two years to attain her present status, and bone-weary exhaustion had begun to take its toll. She had looked forward to coming back to Toronto—taking it easy—until Luke had sprung this CN Tower layout on her, saying that it would be the pièce de résistance of their year's work.

"What are those white things on your hands, love?" Luke asked, a frown appearing on his brow.

Looking down and then up again swiftly, Elizabeth replied, "Those are just my knuckles. I told you, I'm afraid of heights!"

"Yes, but you are going to let go of that rail, aren't you? Come on, Liz, let's have some professionalism. Just one hand then, sweetheart," Luke coaxed. "That's it—put it to your hair. Turn, turn. . .just a wee bit of profile. Got it, got it. . .smile Liz. . .laugh. Did I ever tell you the joke about the knock-kneed model? She went on a crash diet to create a space between her knees and then made it a practice to ride an elephant at least once a day for many years. Well, as you can imagine, the extreme cure made her bowlegged, but by then her breasts had sagged because of age and the rigors of the elephant ride, so it didn't really matter. She was finished, regardless."

"You call that a joke?" Elizabeth asked, though she was tempted to laugh. Luke's "model fables," based as they were on the vanities of the profession, always had that effect on her, despite the fact that one could just as easily cry over the premium placed on a woman's youth and looks in her field. Luke's so-called jokes always seemed to underline that. For twenty minutes, Elizabeth smiled, turned and tossed her head, looked haughty, pensive, troubled. Then she welcomed the camera as she would a long-awaited lover, as it zoomed in for a close-up of her face that, in all its startling beauty, had become the Rawley symbol.

"Ahh," Luke murmured. "The Rawley Girl, at long last. There she is, and she's going to get very passionately kissed. . ."

Holding the pose, Elizabeth said through immobile lips, "And ruin this perfect makeup job? No man would dare."

"Shh. . .I'm covering all bases. Just take one slow step forward, Liz, and part those delicious lips just a touch more. . . . That's it, that's it. . .and hold it. Finis! Wonderful," he said, lifting his head and smiling in self-satisfaction. "I ought to direct movies."

Used to being completely abandoned at the end of a photo session, Elizabeth took Luke's self-congratulatory remarks philosophically. The bravery she felt she had exhibited by letting go of the rail midway through the shooting was not commented on, nor was the fact that she was now shivering with cold because Luke was presently using her "working cape" to tenderly wrap his Nikon. "Doesn't it have its own security blanket?" she asked through chattering teeth, as she hugged her arms against the thin, transparent gown.

"Listen, it's a long way down, and I'm not taking a chance on this baby getting jostled in the elevator. If I hold it like it's a real baby, nobody will get that close."

"You're telling me," Lenny said. "Last time I was in an elevator with one of those critters, it spit up all over me."

"Oh, brother," she said with mock exasperation. "May I have your attention? It might interest you both to know that I have not moved from this spot. And why, you ask?"

"I didn't ask why. Did you ask why, Luke?"

"No." He glanced Elizabeth's way. "Why, Liz?"

"Because I can't! Because if I move one inch, I know I'll be drawn over the edge of this platform into that yawning abyss! But do either of you care?"

"Go get her, Lenny," Luke said absentmindedly, having still not got the folds quite right. "She gets vertigo in high places. I told you to take your Gravol," he said to Elizabeth without looking up.

"I did take my Gravol, and that's why I haven't blacked out yet." She gratefully grasped Lenny the moment he was within reach. She sagged against him as he brought her well in from the edge, feeling both exhaustion and relief wash over her.

"Go on down to the van and get warm," Luke said, finally taking note of her pinched features. "Lenny and I will be a few minutes yet."

Elizabeth entered the indoor observation area gratefully, and was greeted by applause from the onlookers who had been kept behind a barricade.

"That's her! Elizabeth Jackson!" someone said. "Quite a looker, eh?"

"Could I have your autograph, Miss Rawley?" a young girl asked nervously as Elizabeth was passing.

Elizabeth, feeling too weary for this, nonetheless halted and smiled as she took the pad and pen from the girl. "Tell me the truth," Elizabeth said confidentially to the teenager. "Someone had to pay you to come all the way up here, right?"

The girl laughed delightedly. "Oh, no! I came up to see you. And, gosh, you're even more beautiful in person."

"Thank you, but you're a very lovely girl yourself," Elizabeth returned truthfully. "Perhaps you ought to try modeling someday?"

"Do you think I could?" the young girl asked, her eyes alight; she was obviously seeing nothing but the glamour of the profession.

"Yes," Elizabeth said, still shivering a little. "If you're healthy and have lots of stamina. And very warm blood," she finished on a dry note, giving the girl back her pen and pad.

As she entered the elevator, she heard the girl call out, "I'm going to start a fan club for you, Miss Raw—Ms Jackson!"

Elizabeth blew her a kiss as the doors slid shut.

She waited in the van, her head thrown back against the passenger seat and a lap robe drawn up to her chin. She had left the window down a little, feeling as though she needed all the air her lungs could possibly get. There was no doubt about it, she determined, she was really done in.

Closing her eyes, she thought wearily of the necessity of going home to change before taking a taxi to her grandparents' landscaped estate in High Park. As luck would have it, her grandmother had called the instant she had entered her apartment—laden with luggage—earlier in the day. Elizabeth was told to come for tea the moment she was free, and her grandmother had not been prepared to hear anything about jet lag or nervous exhaustion or any other just-got-in-the-door excuses.

"It will have to be a late visit, then," Elizabeth had said, quickly outlining her schedule for the rest of the day.

"Good," her grandmother had replied. "Because I need to talk to you about that mother of yours! And by then, I just might be calm enough to manage it without getting you defensive."

All of which told Elizabeth that she was about to become embroiled in the running battle of wills between Rose Claybourne and Catherine Jackson. And as usual, she would be pulled both ways—her streak of conservatism often allied her with her grandmother, but her mother usually managed to hold sway over her emotions. What would it be this time, she wondered. Politics? Religion? Or perhaps a wild new decor her mother had chosen for the guesthouse? Express purpose: to spite the old dragon!

But her mother, Catherine, was really only a pale imitation of the passionate, lively woman she used to be. Elizabeth had been only thirteen when her parents were divorced but old enough to see the change the ensuing years had wrought on her mother. So much of her identity had been tied up in James Jackson that to Elizabeth it seemed Catherine had been floundering ever since.

"There's a lesson to be had there," she murmured to herself as she rested in the peace and quiet of the van, memories enveloping her.

She saw her father gazing directly into her adolescent face and saying "I'm no good for your mother, and I'm no good for you. So you'll be going to live at your grandmother's house from now on."

In her father's vocabulary, her grandmother had always been "that old dragon," so from a very young age Elizabeth had formed a distinct and rather frightening impression of Rose Claybourne. To think that her father would send her to "the hallowed halls of Dragon Manor," while he roamed the world looking for "the winning game," was a little difficult even for an adoring daughter to take. His compulsive gambling had never really touched her until then. She had stopped calling him Daddy at precisely that moment.

Not that she hadn't remained fond of James over the years—visiting him when the opportunity arose, particularly when he had settled down in Alberta. Staying in the country, he had told her, helped keep his gambling fever under control. "No casinos," he had said with a laugh.

There was a difference between fondness and blind devotion, however, and Elizabeth had learned that a healthy dose of cynicism usually stood one in good stead where James Jackson was concerned.

She really ought to go back for a visit, she mused. It wasn't James's fault that he lived so close to a memory that still had the ability to prickle her skin. But that was silly. Half a dozen years had past, and she had a new image, maturity and a light to medium sprinkle of wisdom and dry humor. What on earth was she afraid of?

Luke and Lenny arrived at the van, Luke with his "baby," though Elizabeth tended to think of it more as his new bride, and Lenny burdened down with all the other equipment. An extension cord hung in coils from his neck, as though Luke had used his head for a game of ring toss.

"How's it going, sleeping beauty?" Luke said, getting in behind the wheel while Lenny squeezed himself in back with all the paraphernalia.

"I was just thinking, Luke. I'm not going to bother going home to change first. I'll be careful of the dress, and I can always return it tomorrow, can't I?"

"You could, I guess. So I suppose you want me to taxi you over to grandma's house?"

"It would save me a lot of time, yes. I'm really beat. Would you mind?"

"Your wish is my command, princess," Luke said, pushing the stick shift into gear.

For a moment, Elizabeth's features hardened, then relaxed as she turned to Luke, commenting dryly, "Well, that's a turn of events, I must say."

Dragon Manor looked much as she had last seen it some months ago—a huge, stately home overrun by ivy, nestled on one and a half acres of sculptured shrubs and manicured lawns. Out of a man-made pond rose a spiraling fountain that recycled the water. Strategically placed spotlights caught the diamond spray, turning the pond into a Disneyland-like focal point, even without the magic of Tinkerbell's wand. This image had gone a long way in curbing her adolescent fears when she had first caught sight of her grandparents' home.

From there it had all been wonderful, for Rose Claybourne had taken one look at her and a smile of joy and appreciation had lit her face. With a glance at Elizabeth's mother, her grandmother had pried her fingers from Catherine's and proceeded to lead her into the mystical realm of Dragon Manor straight to a room that had obviously been prepared for a princess. Elizabeth had stayed awake all night gazing around her in awe, wondering how long she would be allowed to use the room.

Following the summer of her nineteenth year and a trip out west, Elizabeth had looked around the room with distaste and decided not to unpack. But her grandmother's stricken face made her hold on stoically for a further two years, during which time she'd began to pick up modeling assignments. By the time she'd leased her first apartment at the age of twenty-one, she'd been able to support herself fairly adequately. Four years after that, to the day, she was able to command an unheard-of top salary, though she often worked dawn to dusk in the most unlikely locations.

But she had arrived at a deep inner contentment that had little to do with fame and fortune or the fact that possible movie stardom lay just around the corner. All she needed was the courage and faith in herself to reach for it. *And a few hundred more acting lessons*, she told herself as she instructed Luke to drive around to the back of the property.

She was hoping that her mother might be at home in the guesthouse; she was suddenly in the mood for its cozy atmosphere and a chat. Catherine's windows were dark, however, indicating that she'd probably gone out to dinner with friends. No doubt she had not been informed that Elizabeth was home. In this way, her grandmother would be able to air her side of the volcanic argument first. Grandpa, who never took sides or voiced an opinion, would have been allowed to stay.

The back door of her grandmother's house was always unlocked in the off chance that Catherine would wish to pay her respects, and Elizabeth walked directly into the large, incredibly well-equipped kitchen. Aggie the cook was nowhere about, nor was the maid Betty, which precluded a formal announcement of her arrival.

Feeling a little uncomfortable, particularly when she was not expected for some time, Elizabeth walked through the lengthy halls to her grandmother's favorite spot—a sitting room decorated in an Oriental motif. When she heard her grandmother speaking in angry tones, she hesitated just beyond the arched doorway.

"Really, Catherine! You ought to take a leaf out of Elizabeth's book. A more sensible, levelheaded young woman you'll never find. And she's got Charles Durney dancing attendence on her to boot. *The* Charles Durney! And what is her mother proposing to do? Why, she's going to run off and join the circus again!"

Elizabeth, having had no intention of eavesdropping, nonetheless stayed exactly where she was. She had expected to referee a mundane quarrel, but she realized this battle was much more serious.

"James is far more fun than a circus, Mother," Catherine responded drolly.

"Yes, well, I've little doubt he managed to charm you while he was here," Rose returned disdainfully. "Even after all these years, Catherine, you're still so very quick to jump on that particular carnival ride."

"It beats sipping tea with you."

"I detest this type of talk! This is what he has done to you already! It might behoove you to realize that you are a forty-six-year-old woman. Instead you are acting like a—"

"A woman very much in love," Catherine broke in impatiently. "And why do you persist in going over and over this? Do you really think you're going to change my mind? You, of all people? If it hadn't been for your constant badgering—always trying to make me feel guilty where Elizabeth was concerned—I probably would never have left James in the first place. It wasn't as if he ever abused or mistreated us."

"No! He would simply take off in search of Lady Luck and forget he even had a wife and a daughter! How many times were you left behind without even enough food for the two of you to eat? How can you have so easily forgotten what it was like?"

Elizabeth put her hand to her heart when she heard her mother say with extreme emotion, "Because it's been twelve long years! Any life James offered me was better than the stultifying existence here!"

"Catherine! For heaven's sakes, sit down."

"No. Mother, it pleases me to pace for the moment, otherwise I might do something really drastic like throwing that Ming vase. You simply can't get it through your head that James has quit gambling, can you? Nothing I say will convince you, and I don't know why I'm even taking the time to bother."

"A leopard does not change his spots so easily, Catherine. And the reason you are trying to convince me is because you know I'll cut you off without a cent if you go through with this. And then how on earth will you survive in that Sludgewater place of his?"

Sounding as though she were gritting her teeth, Catherine said, "That's Sweetwater, Mother."

Elizabeth remembered when James had told her how the farm in the Kananaskis Valley had come by its name. He had put down roots there after he had acquired a famous stud horse by virtue of an all-night poker game. He had named the horse Dadblastit, for the same sort of fitting reasons he had named the stud farm Sweetwater. "There are some wilderness lakes escaping acid rain," he had explained to her. "And I think I've got the sweetest and purest of them all, right at my back door."

What puzzled her about this whole conversation was how a reconciliation had come about between her mother and James. Had he simply come to Toronto and managed to sweep her mother off her feet again? It certainly sounded that way, and Elizabeth wasn't sure how she felt about it. She had been no different than any other child of divorced parents in hoping that the two people she loved best in the world would one day get together again. But all fantasy aside, she was taking Rose Claybourne's comments into full consideration.

"Sweetwater, Sludgewater, what's the difference? He won it gambling, he'll lose it the same way. Mark my words!"

"It was only a horse he won, Mother. And I'm through with marking your words. James has been making a go of that place for the past eight years, so his gambling must be well under control. In fact, he swears he hasn't sat down at a gaming table for over two years. He even offered me proof."

The older lady sniffed. "What sort of proof?"

"A character reference."

"Easy enough to come by."

"Do you want to hear this or not? Because I really couldn't care less about offering you any sort of proof. I believe James, and that's all that counts. And as for cutting me off without a cent, you should know by now that money means little to me. In any case, James is doing very well. Even if he wasn't, he wouldn't accept financial assistance from you even indirectly if you were the last person on earth."

"I know very well he detests me, and the feeling is mutual. But all right, Catherine. Go ahead and tell me who is supplying this character reference. No doubt neither of us has heard of him."

"You may not recognize the name, but certainly you've heard of the Opal L ranch that borders on James's property."

"Catherine, I know nothing of ranching, other than that it's a dirty, dusty business. Is this ranch of some import?"

Elizabeth had involuntarily taken a quick step away from the doorway, as if the conversation had suddenly become physically dangerous. Her entire body had stiffened at the mention of the Opal L.

"You could say that, yes. It's one of the few remaining open-range ranches. That makes it both enormous and very well-known. The man who owns it is considered a cattle baron, Mother. That should sit very well with you. Elizabeth could no doubt tell you more about him since, apparently, she spent a great deal of time at his ranch when she used to visit James every summer. The point is he's very well respected, very well-known in certain circles, and he certainly wouldn't stake his reputation on James if this was all a sham."

"Elizabeth knows him, you say?"

"Yes. I knew that would get your attention," Catherine responded. "My darling daughter can never do wrong in your eyes, can she?"

Elizabeth felt more than a little hurt at the tone of her mother's voice.

"Instead of making snide comments you should thank your lucky stars you managed to produce a daughter like Elizabeth."

"Snide? Don't be ridiculous. It's just that sometimes I wish Elizabeth would let down her hair. She's altogether too much like you, Mother, in spite of that glamorous career of hers. And doesn't it seem to you that, well, where men are concerned, they leave her cold? Oh, I know, I know—she has the wondrous Charles Durney at her beck and call. I'm not saying he isn't a lovely man, but I'll bet you anything she isn't sleeping with him."

"And you consider that a flaw." Rose said with heavy sarcasm. "She's waiting until she gets his ring on her finger. I consider that smart."

"No. That isn't it at all. I don't think Elizabeth has any plans to get married. I...I just worry about her, that's all. I don't think she's as happy as she pretends to be."

"Nonsense. Elizabeth simply knows better than to fall at a man's feet the way you are apt to do. She has her pride and her dignity. And as I said before, Catherine, you should take a leaf out of her book! Sometimes I wonder who is the younger and who is the older. I intend to fill Elizabeth in on this foolishness when she arrives. Maybe she'll be able to talk some sense into you. Heaven knows I can't."

"Elizabeth will tell you that Logan is neither a fool nor a liar, so—"

"Who? Who is this Logan person? The so-called cattle baron?"

"Not so-called! His full name is John Logan, but for some reason or another, everyone simply refers to him as Logan. According to James, it has something to do with..."

Elizabeth reached the safety of the kitchen with a sense of relief, knowing there was no way she was going to become embroiled in this particular argument. She would hail a cab, and then once safely behind the closed and locked door of her apartment, she would telephone her regrets. To be placed in the position of vouching for Logan was simply too much to ask of her at the present time—at any time.

And were James and her mother going to remarry? The prospect was difficult to cope with rationally. As usual, she was of two minds on the issue. James loved her mother with a passion—that she knew. But in the final analysis, gambling had always come first, and so Elizabeth found it difficult to believe that he had really given it up.

But if Logan said so, then it had to be true. *Logan.* She had not consciously thought of him for many years. Not until today, after the photo session. Maybe that time track she had been stuck on today had been a portent of sorts.

On the ride home in the taxi, despite the uncomfortable things her mother had said about her, Elizabeth found her heart going out to Catherine. They needed to meet and talk one on one, she realized. It had been too long since they had really talked. She wanted so much for her mother to be happy, and James had always seemed to hold the key to that.

"I'M HOME, DARLING," Elizabeth said, the phone to her ear as she perched on the edge of her velvet sofa. The robe she wore was old and a bit shabby, but it had become a sort of security blanket over the years. Elizabeth always found herself putting it on when she was especially troubled about things.

"Do you realize what you just called me?" Charles replied, soft pleasure in his voice.

"I...Charles, do you realize you have a very stuffy name?"

"Princely, they tell me."

"Well, you're an absolutely sweet, laid-back darling, and I think I'm about to tell the world."

"Elizabeth, my heart's beating awful hard here. What's got into you, my love?"

"It's been two long months since I've seen you, Chuck."

"Chuck?"

"Chuckles? Charles. I simply cannot go on calling you Charles. Don't you have any nicknames?"

"Well, an old girlfriend of mine used to call me sweet cheeks."

"How come? Or shouldn't I ask?"

"Depends how intimate you want this conversation to be."

"You do look kind of cute from the rear, come to think of it."

"So do you. I'm coming over, Liz."

"Er, no, Charles. You can't come over just yet."

"Why? Elizabeth, I need to catch you when you're in the mood. Do you realize I haven't looked at another woman since I met you? I'm alone twiddling my thumbs half the time, and you, dear girl, won't even give me something to remember you by."

"I have this absolutely marvelous evening planned for tomorrow night, Charles. So be a good boy and wait, because I'm an utter mess now."

"You? A mess? That's hard to believe. But tell me about this 'marvelous evening.'"

"I thought we might have a picnic on my thick, luxurious, nearly brand-new carpeting."

"Interesting. Go on."

"I plan on preparing stuffed mushrooms, escargots, deep-fried cheese balls and zuchinni. And for the main course..."

"You've named all my favorite hors d'oeuvres. Don't disappoint me now, luscious girl."

"The main course is me, Charles. Or should I say, sweet cheeks?"

After a long silence, Charles came back with, "I don't believe this, but I'm becoming a bundle of nerves here, anyway. What if I don't measure up after all this time?"

"Have I ever made you feel inadequate, Charles?" Elizabeth asked, frowning to herself.

"No. But there's always a first time."

"You, Charles? Why, you're Canada's finest. Just ask my grandmother."

"But I don't want to sleep with your grandmother, sweetheart."

Elizabeth laughed. "You aren't turning me down here, are you?"

"Lord, no."

"Charles, did I ever tell you about my wallflower days in high school?"

"Wallflower? With your looks?"

"My looks are what did it, I guess. Nobody would ask me out for a date because they automatically assumed I would turn them down. There were days, Charles, when I prayed for an outbreak of acne. Then came the day I woke up with a pimple on my chin. With the blemish and a pair of blue jeans, which I had hidden away in my closet so that my grandmother wouldn't throw them out, I prepared for school just knowing that Gordy Spencer would surely stop and talk to me in the hall. Gordy was the jock to end all jocks—big, muscle-bound, you know. All the girls flipped over him."

Charles was chuckling. "So what happened?"

"My grandmother caught sight of me as I was slinking out the door. She took one look at my chin and marched me straight to the doctor. Can you believe that, Charles? By the next morning my face was clear, and my grandmother had disposed of the jeans and bought me a pair of jodpurs instead. Jodpurs!"

"Poor little rich girl," Charles sympathized.

"If it hadn't been for the visits out west, where my father made sure to keep a supply of jeans on hand for me, denim would never have touched this well-cared-for skin. Grandmother always claimed that it chafed something awful."

"You're getting me aroused here. Nothing between you and your Calvins, eh?"

"That's not my commercial spot, thank goodness."

After a moment of silence, Charles spoke hesitantly. "I love you, Liz. I hope you know that."

"Of course. Do you think I'd offer this bod to just anybody?"

"No jokes. I can't wait to see you and tell you how much I care."

"I'll be looking forward to seeing you, too, Charles."

"Why don't we have lunch tomorrow, too? You're all through for the summer, right?"

"Yes, but I'm hoping to get together with my mother for lunch tomorrow. She—I really need to talk to her about something."

"You sound worried."

"I am. I'll tell you all about it tomorrow evening, all right?"

"All right, love. Sweet dreams, gorgeous."

"Good night, Chuckles."

Take that, Mother, Elizabeth thought with a wry little twist to her lips as she hung up. One of them was laboring under a delusion and it wasn't she. She was as happy as a clam and as normal as rainfall. And Charles was not stuffy.

Shortly after her phone call to Charles, exhaustion prodded her into her soft, comfortable bed. "There's no place like home. There's no place like home," she murmured, as she lay back luxuriously against the plumped pillows. "Turn off the light, Aunty Em..."

Through heavy eyelids she regarded the array of Rawley cosmetics standing like tin soldiers on her dressing table, ready for quick but deft application whenever the occasion called for it. She had unpacked them earlier, but had neglected to put the jars and bottles in any kind of order. Her eyes closing now, she remembered that she had also neglected to apply night moisturizer, but knew that there was absolutely no way she was going to climb out of bed to put it on. Let her skin dry up and become old and wrinkled before its time, she thought drowsily, reaching out with great effort to turn off the table lamp. She had the entire summer free of being a dress-up doll.

"Your wish is my command, princess," Luke had said, and if it had not been for the unbearable collage of memories that statement had drummed up, she could have really laughed at that. And Luke knew better. He knew the work and effort that went into looking stunning for the camera. Luke knew. But she supposed men like Logan would still consider hers a pampered existence.

She turned into her pillow and squeezed her eyes tightly shut to help blot out the memories, but they were coming fast and furiously now, and with them, a tight, squeezing sensation gripped her heart. Added years and a certain amount of sophisticated living could only take a person so far, it seemed. Sooner or later the mind and emotions required a therapeutic wallow into one's vulnerable past—complete with sounds, smells and Technicolor images. She could step into the images and go with the flow, as it were, or she could continue to fight it by keeping herself in this taut, bow-string condition. But that was stupid. She was a big girl now. And who needed this clutter? Best to relive that last scene with Logan, with all the pathetic details intact. After all, the time might soon come when she'd have to meet him face-to-face, and if that had to happen she intended to do it with her emotions fully contained. No more would she react to the mere mention of his name or to an errant memory. It was simply a matter of wiping the slate clean with a thorough finality.

She exhaled a long breath, relaxed her body and went forth with only a little hesitation into her most vivid memory. Pain and mortification had given it that extra edge....

"LIZ'BETH," he said, his soft drawl brushing against the nerve endings of her exposed nape. "If you wanted to douse me with beer, you should have done it before Kate sat down beside me. As it is, she got the worst of it, and I'm still... undampened."

There it was again. Sensual nuances in his tone and in his words. It was as if he was holding out a ripe plum to her. Yet she knew if she were to turn and reach out for it, it would immediately become sour and unpalatable. He would give her this much, but only if she kept her distance. She had learned this well.

A horse whickered in the nearest stall as he moved closer, giving her sufficient warning to prepare for his nearness, possibly his touch. Her slim shoulders stiffened and then remained still beneath the warmth of his palms. She closed her eyes and willed herself not to respond, particularly when he lowered his voice.

"Why did you do it?" he asked, as if expecting she were capable of intelligent speech.

She could catch his scent now, and if she just took very small inhalations he would not know how deeply she was indulging herself—how the blend of horses and leather and tobacco had become an aphrodisiac to her. Her nipples pushed against the fine silk of her blouse. For no sane reason she could think of, she had opted to go braless that day.

"Elizabeth, turn around and look at me."

Impossible. She shook her head slightly, and her hair, though cut in a shorter style for the summer, still swirled and glinted in the dim lighting. A moment or two later, she felt something brush against it, and she made an attempt to persuade herself that it had been his lips.

"It wouldn't have had anything to do with the comment I made about your age, would it?" he asked, his voice coaxing. "I was only concerned about you drinking too much."

"Why?" she finally responded, but was unable to stop the throaty catch in her voice. "Why concern yourself about me? You usually try to ignore my very existence."

"I could never ignore you, princess. No man could."

She felt her teeth clench and then she was able to turn and face him, the blue fire of her eyes sweeping the path clear and enabling her to make contact with the steady, amber gaze of her dreams.

"Don't patronize me," she said bitterly. "Why did you come after me, anyway, Logan? Did you think you could make me feel better by patting my head? Well, I don't need a boy scout," she finished on a low, throbbing note.

"A boy scout," he repeated, a hint of amusement touching the gaze that was taking in her flushed features.

"So it would seem," she tossed back, pleased by his slightly pained expression.

"What do you need then, Liz'beth?" he asked, as if unaware that such a question would immediately throw her into a quandary.

"I..." Color enhanced the contours of her cheeks as she attempted to drag her eyes away from that firm male mouth. "I think you know."

She watched his gaze fall then, first to the soft fullness of her lips, then, as if his peripheral vision had suddenly been caught, to the turgid little peaks under her blouse.

Her breath caught in her throat and her pulse beat off the seconds it took him to raise his eyes to hers once again. Then she was staring at him, staring at a face that had become blank and impassive, denying the temptation her body had offered him.

It was that face she had so often seen when their eyes made contact—the face he never showed to Kate. It was from there her jealously had grown. Kate, who came and went on the ranch as she pleased, who shared jokes and laughter with him, who always became curiously silent whenever Elizabeth appeared.

I've worn my heart on my sleeve and so they laugh at me, she had thought torturously, just before the full beer mug she had been holding seemed to tip of its own accord. And it had really been no accident that Kate got the worst of it.

Looking at the implacable man, she felt hatred. Just once she wanted to break through the mask and have him admit to what she knew so well deep in her feminine soul. How many times had she felt his eyes following her? How many times had her skin turned warm, alerting her to his presense? Sometimes she felt that the intensity of their mutual attraction was palpable. An electric current that sizzled and crackled whenever they were close. She wouldn't let him deny it any longer.

She brought trembling fingertips to the top pearl button of her blouse and undid it. The next two took only a little more effort.

"What are you doing?" Logan asked, his brows beginning to draw together.

"Actions speak louder than words, don't they, Logan?" Trying to control the nervousness that laced her system, she went to work on the next two buttons, aware that she had his undivided attention.

"I can't let you do this, Elizabeth," he cautioned in a strained voice.

"How will you stop me?" She pulled the blouse from the waistband of the jodhpurs she wore—her grandmother's idea of what a well-dressed cowgirl should wear after the sun went down—not daring to look up at him for fear of the flat rejection she might see in his face. Impulsiveness had given way to regret, and she knew she was very near to tears, but she didn't know how to stop without looking even more foolish.

When the last button was released and her blouse hung open, Elizabeth knew she could go no further. One tear and then two hit the straw-littered floor, and then Logan's arms were catching her to him, and she was heaving and hiccupping against his chest as the floodgates opened. It took her several tear-drenched moments to realize that she was exactly where she'd always wanted to be when he began to stroke her hair.

With a sense of wonder, she felt the touch of his mouth on her brow, and then his warm breath was in her ear, his voice saying something tender and soothing. Her arms tight around his waist, she threw her head back to offer him her lips.

She saw that his gaze was indeed on her trembling mouth, but there was a familiar look in his eyes that told her he was about to close up on her, denying them both all over again.

"Why?" Her voice shook with emotion. "Why can't you kiss me? I...I know you think I'm too young for you, but..." She took a ragged breath. "Logan, I'm not. I'm not, and I can prove it to you." She reached up and touched her soft lips against his chin and then his cheek. "If only you'll let me." She ventured now to the corner of his mouth, feeling almost delirious when he did not draw away.

"Logan...Logan...I love you," she breathed huskily, and now she brought his hand down from her hair to touch her lips to the callused palm before pressing it tightly against the parted edges of her blouse. Closing her eyes she murmured, "You can't pretend to me. You can't. I know your eyes follow me constantly."

His voice, normally so soft and liquid, sounded raspy in his reply. "Maybe I can't deny that. But, Liz'beth, you don't want this. For all sorts of reasons."

"I do," she affirmed, shifting his hand. "Logan, feel my heart."

He made a deep, impatient sound as he took his hand away, and then he was releasing her entirely as he said, "Not on your sweet life. Elizabeth, put an end to the seduction scene, all right? It isn't doing either of us any good."

She held her chin up. "Because you're fighting it for some obscure reason."

"Obscure?" He dragged his hand through his hair briefly. "Try my friendship with your father for starters."

"James has nothing to do with us," she declared firmly.

"There is no us, Elizabeth. Try and get that through your head. And do up your blouse while you're at it. I'm telling you this for your own good."

"Are you? I think it's because you're so strongly tempted, Logan," she replied, refusing to have things end like this.

"Elizabeth," he warned, just as she turned her back on him and removed her blouse entirely.

She balled it up, looked back over her shoulder and threw it at him. "Tell me you have no desire at all to look at me."

"No, I won't tell you that. But if I'm really to get a good look at you, why don't you turn around and take off those silly jodhpurs while you're at it."

She felt a blush suffuse her entire body. Through trembling lips, she ordered him to give her back her blouse. She flinched when she felt him directly behind her, and then started when he picked up her arm to thread it through the sleeve of her blouse.

"Don't struggle," he ordered in a tight voice, as he brought back her other arm and pushed it into the other sleeve. Then the blouse was up over her shoulders and he was turning her around with his expression cast in stone as he quickly drew the edges together and did up every last button.

"You see, Liz'beth," he said quietly when he was done, "your age does tend to work against you from time to time."

"I hate you," she bit out. "All I wanted—"

"I know what you wanted" he broke in tautly. "But experiment on another man, okay? Learn to know what's best for you!"

"I thought I did!" she said, with bitter tears in her eyes. "Despite the fact that you're heartless and emotionless!"

His eyes flickered, and for just an instant she caught a look of such burning intensity it made her heart skip a full beat. But it was gone when he said, "Why? Because I'm able to resist all this?" His eyes indicated her face and form. "You're a beautiful girl, Elizabeth, and you must know that pretty well. A man has to clench his teeth when he looks at you." He smiled a little grimly. "Even a man who wears the stench of cattle as his regular cologne. Maybe him especially."

"Why are you telling me this?"

"To explain away the attraction that you won't let me deny. I think I'm a novelty to you, Liz'beth—and vice versa, no doubt. But any fool can see we don't belong together. Look at the floor, sweetheart. It's straw covered and dirty—silk and satin sheets are at a premium out here." He looked at her steadily to make sure she understood his full meaning. "Drawing-room manners, as well."

Her hiccups had returned while he had been speaking, and as she brought her hand up to brush at her wet face, her chest heaved convulsively. "I know you're just trying to scare me off," she said to him, her large eyes looking wise.

He groaned softly. "You're assuming I have a little restraint left—but you're pushing it to the limits, Elizabeth. So what is it going to take to get through to you?"

"*The truth*," she said on a broken sob.

He made an impatient sound. "You've been hearing it—but, all right, I'll go a little further. You're young, all right. Younger than a nineteen-year-old should be. I think it's on account of your looks and your moneyed, high-brow background. You've been spoiled and petted and pampered for a good portion of your life, haven't you?"

"Logan," she whispered, her eyes looking stricken and wounded.

"Liz'beth, don't look at me like that. I'm trying very hard here to make sure that nothing like this happens again. God knows if you were mine I'd spoil you a little, too. But you aren't, and that's never going to happen, so just listen to me. I think the idea of a man's rejection is a little beyond your scope, so I'll put it real plain. I wouldn't touch you with a ten-foot pole if I could help it, but I'm as red-blooded as the next man and one of these days I'm not going to be able to stick to that. Do you understand me, Elizabeth? I want you to take all those newly awakened needs of yours and go back where you came from. There are worlds out there for you to conquer, but as far as mine is concerned, I want you to leave me in peace, before you even begin to realize your full potential. God knows I won't stand a chance then. But I don't need or want those kinds of complications. And you don't need or want the kind of life I have to offer you. So run—don't walk, Elizabeth—just run to the nearest exit. Will you?"

It had become so very difficult to breathe, and a roaring sound was beginning to fill her ears, making it difficult to hear his next statement.

"And while you're at it, Liz'beth, think about forebears—the difference between yours and mine."

Which held no meaning for her because it took all her concentration to stand there with her head held high, while she fought to control the trembling of her chin. Running—or walking—seemed out of the question, and she wished that the ground would simply open up and take her from his sight, for she had no idea how to get from where she stood to the doorway of the barn.

An earthquake, she prayed. Then they would both simply have to run for it—out into the open night where a fissure might open up and swallow her.

She'd had no idea that shattered illusions could hurt so much. She brought her hand to her midriff, feeling the physical pain of his rejection. But then she caught Logan's concerned look and feared the pity she might glimpse in his face. She took her hand quickly away and simply hoped that she would not throw up right in front of him—her coup de grace.

Keeping her chin up and her shoulders level, she somehow managed the careful walk to the dark, comforting square of night without disgracing herself. Once through the door, she turned to look at him, knowing the darkness was an effective cloak for the pain that now wrenched her face.

The last she saw of him—a haunting vision that remained with her for many years—he was standing with his arms at his sides, jaw clenched tightly, amber eyes glittering with a suppressed emotion she was afraid to even decipher.

She ran off into the darkness, putting as much space between herself and the barn as possible, before giving in to her body's demands. The bile tasted of stale beer and a young girl's impossible dreams. She began walking again keeping a tight rein on her emotions—a walk that eventually moved her out of the darkness into a blazing circle of light.

It took precisely six years of space and time.

2

SHE FELT BOTH PURGED AND RESTED when she met her mother for lunch at Truffles the following day. They kissed and embraced, drew back to look at each other with discerning eyes, and then sat down to quickly dispense with the business of reading menus. Catherine ordered champagne cocktails for the two of them.

She was radiant: her eyes glowed, her cheeks were delicately flushed and her mouth looked softly vulnerable. A beautiful, cashmere sweater dress and a new upswept hairdo gave her a fragile Dresden-doll look.

Elizabeth felt her heart expand and then contract. She tried to tell herself that she wasn't scared to death for her mother; she was only feeling a little uneasy.

"Dearest girl," Catherine said, looking at her daughter with undisguised wonder. "How did I manage to give birth to such a ravishing creature? And is it my imagination? Or are your eyes even a deeper shade of blue these days? How can that be?"

Glad to skirt around more important things for the moment, Elizabeth touched the tip of her finger to her eye. "Blue-tinted contacts," she said with a grin.

"Will wonders never cease? You don't actually need them, do you?"

Elizabeth nodded. "Yes, I do. My wide-eyed myopic appeal turned out to be a result of nearsightedness. Luke felt we could compensate for losing the look by deepening my eye color."

"You do look fabulous—older and wiser somehow, too."

Elizabeth slanted Catherine a heavy-lidded look. "This is the latest, Mother. Sultry and exotic. It sells cosmetics like mad."

"I shouldn't wonder. My daughter is becoming a sex goddess."

Elizabeth blew at her nails. "Charles thinks so."

Catherine laughed. "She's developing a wonderful sense of humor, too. Elizabeth, my darling girl, I wish you and I could spend more time together. You've been so busy these past few years that we hardly ever get to see each other."

"Well, I've managed to get this entire summer off, Mother. So you and I will be able to spend more time together." Elizabeth waited for her mother's response, but the champagne cocktails arrived, further delaying it.

Elizabeth picked up her glass by the stem.

"No, Elizabeth, don't drink yet," her mother said, as though on cue. "There's something I'd like to tell you first. It's just that I'm having a little trouble knowing where to begin."

"But what does my cocktail have to do with it?"

"Well, hopefully you'll want to make a toast."

"Champagne cocktails did seem to indicate a special event," Elizabeth said, hoping to make it easier for her mother.

"Then I guess I'm just going to blurt it right out. Oh, Elizabeth," Catherine continued in a rush. "Hold on to your seat because I'm very tempted to ask you to be a witness at a marriage. But if this marriage takes place, it will be out west. West of Calgary, to be more precise," Catherine finished, waiting for her daughter to look puzzled and then dumbstruck.

Elizabeth had not put in years of practice before the camera for nothing; she managed both expressions amazingly well. "You don't mean...You can't mean...You and James?"

Her mother nodded happily. "I knew you'd be rocked. But Elizabeth, don't you think it's high time? You know we've never stopped loving each other. You know that better than anyone; you you used to visit James so often."

"Used to, Mother," Elizabeth answered carefully, not wishing to make her mother defensive as her grandmother had done. "You have to remember that I haven't been out there for quite a few years now...being so busy with my career and all," she added, in case her mother questioned her on that as she had once before.

"Yes, I know. But you still talk to James long distance, and I know the two of you have always written. I...I never wanted to ask you this before, Elizabeth. It was too painful a topic, I guess. But, well, James must have spoken of me often to you..."

Her mother trailed off, hoping Elizabeth would know what she was asking. Elizabeth filled the gap truthfully, for James's love for her mother had never been at issue. "He's always talking about you, Mother."

Catherine's eyes grew moist. "I knew that, of course. But for some reason I needed you to tell me what I already knew. Your grandmother and I had a terrific row about it yesterday afternoon, and it started up again in the evening. So it was just as well you didn't come. You should have heard the derogatory things she was saying about James. I knew I shouldn't have told her about it. You weren't here, though, and I guess I had to blurt my happiness out to someone. *Poor choice!*"

"I can imagine," Elizabeth said quietly.

"So what do you think? Are you happy for me?"

"I'm happy for you both. But, Mother, you're going to have to give me a chance to take this in. I mean how...how soon are you expecting to marry James?"

Catherine frowned a little, but it wasn't in response to her daughter's question. "I know I've never objected before to your calling your father James, but it does seem to me that now we're going to be together again you ought to...well, address him accordingly."

Elizabeth looked at her mother for several seconds before managing a response. "Then it really is a fait accompli?"

Catherine nodded. "He proposed while he was here in Toronto, and after giving it careful thought, I accepted. I didn't tell your grandmother this, of course, so it's just between you and me. She thinks I'm going out there to sort of prejudge the situation. You know to what I'm referring?"

"Yes." There seemed little that she could add in view of the fact that her mother's features had taken on a definite notrespassing look.

"James has quit gambling and that's all that needs to be said."

"Is it?" Elizabeth dared to question.

Catherine's lips tightened. "I suppose you don't believe it," she stated. "There are times, Elizabeth, when you are my mother all over again."

"I'm sorry," Elizabeth said, apologizing for such a flaw. "It's just that I'm worried about how you would take a slipup on Jame—on Dad's part. In view of the fact that you seem so certain about marrying him again."

"There isn't going to be any slipup," Catherine answered with certainty. "James would never hurt me like that again. And besides, it's my life, Elizabeth. So the decision is mine. I did hope that you would be happy for me, though," her mother finished, looking a little betrayed.

Elizabeth saw that any further references to her father's gambling would not only be useless, they wouldn't be tolerated. In addition, she felt that if she didn't make the effort here and now to show unrestrained happiness for her mother there was a good possibility that Catherine would get up and walk out of the restaurant.

Picking up her champagne cocktail in preparation to extend all best wishes, Elizabeth reflected on the fact that woman head over heels in love was an entirely unreasonable creature and had to be treated gently in accordance with that. A woman in love was the most vulnerable person on earth.

"SO WHEN IS SHE FLYING OUT THERE?" Charles asked from the depths of the thickly carpeted conversation pit. He was propped against several scatter pillows, a glass of red wine in his hand.

Elizabeth folded up their tablecloth as she said, "In four weeks."

"A moon, eh?"

"So the pagan story goes."

"And you think she's going to marry him right away?"

"She asked me to come along for that express purpose. Then, of course, she wants me to get lost, three being a crowd where newlyweds are concerned. She suggested I stay with a friend of James's, who apparently has offered to open his home for the nuptuals. But I would rather fly home directly afterward."

"Then all the plans have been made?"

"Definitely. Can you believe it?"

"You don't think your father's really given it all up, do you?"

"An alcoholic can fall off the wagon, can't he, Charles? Despite all the best intentions in the world? It's compulsive, and that's how I view my father's gambling. I'd like to believe that it couldn't ever happen, that he wouldn't put cards or dice before my mother's happiness again. But common sense tells me that if he could have quit so easily, he would have done it long ago. After all, they've been apart for twelve years, Charles."

"During which time he's maybe gotten older and wiser? Tobacco addiction can be a lifelong habit, too, yet there are plenty of strong-minded people who have managed to break it before it does them in entirely. But they choose their own time, Elizabeth. Quitting can't be forced on them. Then the magic day comes when they look at their pack with disgust and throw the damned things away."

"I hardly think you can compare this with smoking."

"No? I've known smokers who can't give it up even when their emphysema has been diagnosed. So don't belittle the addiction—it's a powerful one. The question you have to ask yourself is, how strong-willed is James?"

"Very—except where gambling is concerned."

"Okay, so he needed to choose his own time. And worrying about this isn't going to do you the least bit of good. You might as well try looking on the bright side."

Elizabeth picked up her empty wineglass and extended it to Charles.

"That was good, Charles—what you said, I mean. Now all I need is a little more of the grape to become truly relaxed."

Charles twirled an imaginary mustache as he poured her glass full. "Get drunk, okay? We don't want any ol' inhibitions getting in the way."

Elizabeth took a hefty sip and then slowly licked her lips in a very sensual manner as she carefully settled herself down beside him.

Charles moaned a little as she continued to drink the rest of her wine in the same way, not relinquishing the glass until every drop was gone. Charles's full glass remained where it was on the ceramic hearth.

"Inhibitions all gone," she told him, passing him the glass. "How's your performance anxiety?"

"I think I just might pass the test," Charles said, taking her into his arms with purposeful, no-nonsense intent.

"I knew you were too good-looking to be shy," she murmured, as their lips met in a soft kiss.

"Love has given me wings," he said, moving to touch his lips to her cheek, to her eyelids, and then down to leave a soft trail against her throat.

"It's also given you good technique."

"You might be a sophomore, darling, but I...I am a senior."

"Even at that, I think I've acquired credits here that I haven't earned."

"Now is not the time for reflections or comparisons. Lord knows I'm not up to that," he confessed softly against the lobe of her ear.

"Fear not. Believe me, Charles. Fear not. I've made love to exactly two men in my life, and neither time was it a momentous occasion. So I decided to give it up before it became habit-forming in any way. Does that put your mind at ease?"

"Not really," he murmured, moving to her lips once again. "But I can't put my finger on why at the moment."

Talking ceased as Charles's ardor increased, his hand moving along the contours of her body now as his mouth parted to take possession of hers.

"I love you, Elizabeth," he breathed, as his lips went to her cheek, her nose, her brow in feathery caresses, then returned to her lips once again. She was conscious of his tenderness, the sincerity of his feelings, and she gave of herself accordingly, feeling that Charles deserved her full response.

He began to undress her, undoing the long zipper of the lounging gown she had slipped into before his arrival at her apartment. Cool air struck her breasts as Charles exposed her to his admiring gaze, and then she was feeling the warm, moist trail of his lips on their fullness. His tongue circled a nipple, and she moaned softly—appropriately—and then became conscious of what she was doing. She had begun to fake her responses.

It wasn't fair to Charles and it wasn't fair to her. Yet this robot side of herself always seemed to take over during lovemaking. It was the same professional Elizabeth who could make love to a camera or an imaginary television audience—whatever the occasion called for. And this particular occasion required that she make love with Charles.

Because he was the best man on earth, and yes, she did love Charles, which meant she had no explanation for her lack of physical feeling. She felt warm and wanted and that was all very nice, but...

The phone rang sharply, the noise startling them both to the extent that Charles's full glass of wine overturned, its contents spreading onto Elizabeth's carpet. She wanted to cry at the sight but managed to contain herself.

Charles frowned at the ringing phone and then looked down at the stain as he got to his knees. "Damn! Darling, I'm sorry," he said, shouldering the full blame for the mishap. "I'll buy you a new carpet."

"Don't be absurd," she said, swiftly using the tablecloth to soak up as much of the spillage as possible. Charles could replace the entire contents of her apartment building without even noticing a drop in funds, so unless she was very firm about it, a six-hundred-square-foot carpet would be arriving with the sun in the morning. "You could get the phone, though," she said, softening her tone and throwing him a smile over her shoulder.

While Charles picked up the phone, Elizabeth ran to the kitchen, thinking of the many hours of work that had gone into the purchase of her pale mauve carpet, which was presently sporting a large purple stain. Despite a top salary, she would need a large chunk of her earnings to replace it. She was almost tempted to let Charles do his thing.

But she was nobody's pampered darling, she reminded herself, as she emerged from the kitchen with her arms full of every conceivable remedy from vinegar to baking soda.

Charles held the phone out to her as she passed. "Not now, Charles," she moaned. "Ask whoever it is to phone back."

Charles put his mouth to the phone and repeated the message while Elizabeth fell to her knees in front of the stain.

"He says he'll hold," Charles said a moment later, with a wry smile on his face. "Until you're all through with whatever breathless thing you're doing."

Luke, Elizabeth thought with annoyance, wondering what spur-of-the-moment thing he'd come up with now. These were her holidays, dammit!

"Tell him," she said, past the vinegar fumes, "that he's caught us in an inspirational moment. Tell him that a balancing act on the CN Tower is nothing compared to this. And tell him that this time I don't even need my Gravol."

"Okay," Charles said obligingly. "But shouldn't I ask who it is first?"

"I know who it is. Just repeat the message please, and then tell him to get lost."

"Okeydokey." Charles cleared his throat and then repeated the message word for word.

"Who me?" he said after a brief moment. "My name's Durney. What's yours, friend?"

"Well, glad to make your acquaintance, but you did knock over my wine, John. Poor Liz is presently on her hands and knees on account of it. Give me your number and I'll have her get back to you, all right? But you should bear in mind she's already spoken for."

"That's about it, friend...so maybe you can tell me what this call is all about?"

By this time, Elizabeth was looking up with a frown. *John?* she thought. She didn't know any John, although she had met a movie producer by that name when she and Luke were in the States. But there were an awful lot of Johns in the world, and she had told that one in particular that she had no urge yet to make a fool of herself on the silver screen, having had no real training as an actress. But wouldn't it be just her luck to give such a message to someone of future import?

Charles was frowning now as he began to jot something down on the telephone pad, bringing Elizabeth slowly to her feet as a premonition crept over her. She suddenly knew who it was and why he was calling. She moved over to Charles.

"Hold the phone," he said. "I think I'd better put her on, after all." Covering the mouthpiece, he said to Elizabeth, "Someone called John Logan. He says it concerns your father."

3

ELIZABETH DIDN'T KNOW which she dreaded most: hearing what had befallen her father, or hearing once again the sound of Logan's voice. It was definitely a toss-up, she thought, as she gingerly took the receiver from Charles.

"Don't jump to conclusions," he warned, seeing the stricken look on her face. "It might not be that at all."

She looked at Charles in an uncomprehending way and then turned slightly away from him as she brought the instrument to her ear. She became aware of her unzipped gown and the sudden warmth that was creeping through her as she gathered herself to speak. She brought the unzipped edges together protectively with her other hand.

He must have heard the sound of her uneven breathing, for he spoke first.

"Too much exercise can be detrimental to your health, Liz'beth."

She closed her eyes tightly for a moment before replying. "I was simply cleaning up some spilled wine."

"And before that, an inspirational moment I hear."

That warmth was growing causing her palm to sweat with her grip on the receiver. She had an overwhelming urge to hang up and run out of the room. Instead, with great effort, she forced a measure of coolness into her voice. "Charles said you were ringing about my father."

"Charles?" he questioned.

"Durney. He's already introduced himself, I believe."

"And his close relationship to you, as well."

"Get to the point, Logan." *There*, she thought. She was beginning to hit her stride now. That soft, mocking voice of his could go straight to hell.

"All right. You father's in a bad way, Elizabeth."

"In what respect?" She sank down onto the soft sofa cushion.

"In every respect. You want it straight from the shoulder?"

She brought both hands to the receiver. "Yes."

"A little while ago, he looked as though he was going to kill himself. And I was worried enough to decide to spend the night here with him. That's where I'm phoning from, otherwise I wouldn't have minded the long-distance delay in getting you to the phone. James, however, can ill afford it at the moment."

Elizabeth felt her heart sink. So it had happened already, and her father was hating himself as a result. She could have almost written the scenerio.

"How much did he lose?" she asked heavily.

"His shirt. Or rather, the ready cash to buy one. His capital's all cleaned out. He also lost Dadblastit."

"Oh, no," Elizabeth said weakly.

"But more than that, he's lost all faith in himself. I take it you knew about his plans to bring your mother out here?"

"She said he'd proposed to her. Oh, Logan, she even talked about Dadblastit today at lunch, telling me she was anxious to meet a horse with such an unusual name. You...you just can't imagine how she's going to take this."

"Yes, I can. Why else would he want to shoot himself?"

Elizabeth nearly dropped the phone. "He actually...?"

"That was the picture when I walked in here. Good thing I came over."

"But James doesn't own a gun!" she said in protest, not wanting to believe what Logan was saying. Charles immediately came over to her side, looking horrified. Elizabeth shook her head at him in a silent message.

"He went out and bought one right after the big private game. Poker, of course. James figures he's an expert there."

Elizabeth put her hand to her brow. *Why now,* she thought. Apparently he'd managed to stay away from gambling for so long. Why slip up on the brink of his remarriage to her mother? Aloud, she said "Wasn't it true, then, Logan? James had told Mother he had quit, and that you would back him up in that."

"I know." She heard him sigh heavily. "What can I say? I feel largely responsible for all this. Maybe your mother would have turned him down if he hadn't offered my name as proof. All I can say is, I believed James had given it all up. He still claims that's true, that last night was the first time."

"Did Mother ever contact you about it?"

"No. I guess the fact that James had proof was enough for her. I did receive a phone call from your grandmother, though—Rose Claybourne?"

Elizabeth felt no real surprise at this. "When did she call?"

"Last night while James was out doing his bad deed. Of course I didn't know about it then, so I told her that as far as I was concerned, James was a reformed man."

"Did she believe you?"

"No," Logan said flatly. "She said I didn't sound like a fool, but obviously I was. I began to understand why James calls her the dragon. Unfortunately, though, the lady was right."

"It was kind of you to involve yourself in this." Elizabeth felt she had to say that. "On James's behalf, I mean. You were trying to do him a favor."

"One that backfired, I'm afraid. Anyway, I don't really know what to do about all this. I plied James with booze until he got numb enough to sleep, and as I said, I'll stay here for the night. Hopefully, in the morning I can talk him into coming back to the ranch with me, because right now we're just finishing spring roundup, and I'm needed here. But beyond that, I don't know if I can really be of much help to him. He's a broken man, Elizabeth."

"I'll come immediately," she said in response. "I'll catch the first flight in the morning."

Logan did not speak for a long moment, and she was on the brink of questioning him when she heard "Good."

Once again she was conscious of a flushed and heated feeling—a direct response to that one softly uttered word.

"You and James will stay at the ranch," he went on, and he suddenly sounded like the old Logan to her—self-assured and commanding. "And I'll send Red over to take care of your father's place. Maybe between the two of us—you and me, Elizabeth—we can somehow find a solution to this problem. James needs professional help. I'm going to look into that. In the meantime, you could talk to him and try to find out why he suddenly started gambling again when he's come so far. I have a hunch why, but that's all it is."

Elizabeth felt immense gratitude that Logan was so willing to take charge and help out with the situation—but she knew those sorts of feelings were dangerous to her well-being. It was enough that a slight change in his tone could still have this sort of effect on her after so many years. Logan, she realized, comparing her feelings to those of a while ago with Charles, was the only man she had ever really wanted—the irony being that he did not want her back. It paid to keep that clear memory in mind and guard herself accordingly. Otherwise it might well be possible to make a fool of herself all over again. Particularly if she was going to be staying in his home.

"Thank you very much, Logan," she said politely. "Because yes, I could certainly use your help with James. When it comes to Mother, however, I'm on my own. I honestly don't know what to say to her about all this."

"I think it's best to keep this under wraps for a while, at least until James is better able to face himself. When he can do that, he'll tell Catherine himself, no matter how painful it is. James isn't a weak man, except for his gambling, and he's never been afraid to face the consequeneces before. I feel for your mother, but maybe when he's got some professional help, they can start afresh and put this mishap behind them. The man has already made a superhuman effort to reform himself. With a little outside help, I really think he can lick this thing, Elizabeth."

Elizabeth was steadily feeling much better about the whole situation while Logan was speaking. He went on to say, "If James will allow it, I hope to reimburse him for his losses. In fact, I've already sent Red out to buy back the horse from Carruthers, the man who was the big winner last night, so—"

"James will never allow that," Elizabeth put in quickly, knowing her father well in that respect.

"He will if I tell him I intend to charge interest on the loan. Besides, he isn't in any position to refuse me."

"Nevertheless, I would prefer to help out. I have quite a bit of money put away, so I'll make him the loan myself. But since you've likely already acquired the horse, I would very much appreciate it, on James's behalf, if you would simply hold on to him until I can scrape the price together."

"You're talking well over a quarter of a million dollars," Logan said quietly. "That's a full-blooded Arabian."

Elizabeth's jaw dropped. How on earth could the stakes in a mere poker game have been so high?

"We aren't talking about a bunch of the boys getting together for a friendly little game of poker, you know," he explained, as if she had voiced the question aloud. "This was the big time. Every man sitting at that table, apart from James, could afford to lose large amounts without blinking an eye. Nervousness can make a big loser out of you under those circumstances."

Elizabeth now became overwhelmingly conscious of the huge charge this telephone call was adding to her father's tab. "I wish you would have called me collect," she said swiftly. "Logan, it may take me a little longer to get at my money. I've got a lot of it tied up in stocks and bonds. But I want you to promise me not to reimburse James. I know you can afford it, but so can I. And he is my father, after all."

"But I think I have a little more faith in him, Elizabeth."

She did not know how to respond for a moment, finally saying, "This is all irrelevent, since he probably won't accept it from either of us, anyway."

"Which is saying quite a lot for the man, isn't it?"

"I don't need you to point out my father's good qualities!"

"I think we ought to settle all this when you arrive, don't you?"

"Oh, we'll settle it, all right."

"I can hardly wait," he said, the tone of his voice causing the hair at her nape to prickle.

She glanced over at Charles, who, because of the length of the conversation, was watching her with a slight frown creasing his brow.

"Goodbye, Logan," she said firmly.

"I'll check the morning flight schedules and have Hank pick you up at the Calgary airport."

"Fine."

"It's really been nice talking to you again, Liz'beth."

Without making any sort of response, she hung up the phone, for she certainly was not going to return the compliment. She had said her goodbye and that was enough. She looked at Charles and grimaced a little.

"An old flame?" he said.

She shook her head. "Hardly. Just a friend of my father's." Quickly she went on to explain what had occurred.

"Exactly what you were afraid of," Charles commented.

"More or less, yes." She frowned. "Logan, however, does not seem to think I have sufficient faith in my father. I should have told him, once bitten, twice shy. After all, this is the first time he's ever been involved in James's sickness. How dared he sound so superior?"

"Hey, don't get mad at me," Charles said, lifting his hands. "I'm on your side, remember?"

Yes, she thought, studying his face, but he also looked a little disgruntled over the untimely interruption. She supposed she could hardly blame him, though.

"I'll make it up to you when I get back," she said, giving the promise almost automatically.

"When have I heard that before," he was still able to tease. "And how long do I diddle my time away this time?"

"You don't," she said firmly, knowing it was a large exaggeration, anyway. Charles's time was at a premium at best. "You are to go out with the first woman who asks you."

"As long as I don't ask her first, hmm?"

She knew she wasn't really being fair to him, but Charles was simply too nice a man to lose. She had the thought that if she could just exorcise these lingering feelings for Logan, she would be able to give Charles all that he deserved. Once she saw Logan face-to-face, she would know that it was just a schoolgirl crush that she had never quite got over. As a career-minded adult, she could deal with a man like him easily.

She called the airport to arrange a flight and then, turning to Charles, said apologetically, "Six in the morning."

"I didn't suppose you'd be in the mood after hearing the news about your father, anyway," he said, placing his hands on her shoulders.

She leaned into him gratefully. "Still, you're awfully patient, darling," she said, the endearment still sounding strange on her lips.

"That alone will hold me over for two weeks," he murmured, kissing her brow. "Besides, I'm in love with you, and I guess that means I'll wait indefinitely."

"But maybe you shouldn't."

"Let me decide when it's hopeless, okay?"

"Okay," she said, offering her lips with a warmth that brought a gleam of sweat to his brow.

He broke away, saying, "But I'd better get out of here now."

She stopped him at the door. "Can you cash a rather large check for me?" she asked. "Oh, and one other thing," she went on as they made the transaction. "Phone my mother for me, please? Tell her I was called out of town on a last-minute job, but that I'll get in touch with her as soon as I can."

"All right, but I'll be expecting a call from you myself."

"In a day or two," she promised, kissing him more chastely this time as they stood before the open door. When Charles was gone, she crossed the room and made a call to her accountant, a determined look on her face. Logan was very much mistaken if he thought she'd allow any member of her family to become financially indebted to him. Friendship was one thing, a loan of this size quite another. Besides, she would be doing it for her mother, as well.

It gave her a sense of pride to know she had the earned resources to help in this way. She was no one's spoiled little pet, and it would behoove Logan to realize that.

Armed with her Rawley cosmetics case and her Gravol, Elizabeth boarded the CP Air flight for Calgary. She shook her head quickly when the flight attendant came around with the breakfast trays, but did have the foresight to ask for a large dollop of brandy in her morning coffee. By the time she hit her first air pocket, she was light-headed enough not to panic too much. By the time they landed some three hours later, a Madonna-like smile was gracing her face, and her nerves had entirely ceased to plague her.

She made her way gingerly and smilingly down the ramp. Chuckling to herself with light mirth, she made her way along the covered walkway to the airport building and then ducked into a ladies' room to check on her appearance. Her appearance was of prime importance, she recalled. No blue jeans this visit—no trying to fit in where she didn't belong.

"You look good," she told her reflection softly. "But where's your hat?" She frowned at herself before looking down to discover that she was holding it in her hand. It was a straw boater affair, white and lacy looking, with a cobalt-blue silk scarf that served as the band. She noticed that she had allowed the tip of it to trail on the ground. Tsking at herself, she placed and arranged the hat on her head.

In the sun, the confetti weaving would throw a shadow veil over her face, and the vivid blue of the scarf would pick up the exact color of her eyes. The dress she wore was of the same color, made by a famous designer. The low-cut, draped styling of the bodice displayed the soft mounds of her breasts, jutting pertly against the soft fabric. The snug-fitting waistline drew attention to the womanly flair of hips.

It was a dress designed expressly for a man's pleasure, and Elizabeth had been fully aware of this when she had stepped nimbly into it. If revenge was sweet, she considered that she deserved a small taste of it, regardless of her mission. If Logan could look at her dressed like this and not feel a strong sense of regret, then he was probably inhuman.

Her makeup, flawlessly applied, not only enhanced her beautiful features, it looked fresh and natural and kissed by the sun—no mean feat after three hours of wear. Testimony to the product that she advertised. Her full head of freshly shampooed, dark auburn hair looked glossy and bouncy, its shoulder length, complimented by the hat, a perfect frame for her face.

"You'll knock him out of his boots," she told herself, testing her smile for just the right degree of restrained politeness, as she teetered a bit on her three-inch heels.

A lady came out of one of the cubicles and stared at her as she went to a washbasin as far from Elizabeth as possible. Elizabeth, flushing a little as sobriety tried to creep up on her, kept her head high and carefully exited the room.

With her luggage ticket in hand, she went to the waiting area, wondering if Hank would be able to recognize her from the thin, coltlike nineteen-year-old he had last seen. For her part, she felt relatively assured that the ancient-looking cowboy could not have changed very much, except, of course, to have added a few more burned trails to the parched surface of his face. And yet she was pretty certain that he had not yet seen his sixty-fifth birthday and that "gofer" duties would not sit too well with a man who still considered himself to be in his prime, despite advancing decrepitude.

She was wishing that Logan could have come for her—for her bandbox appearance was certainly going to be wasted on Hank. She had no sooner completed the thought than she saw Logan unfolding himself from a plastic lounge chair.

If it were not for her tranquilized state, Elizabeth had the distinct feeling she might have done something utterly ridiculous, such as bolting from the room, regardless of the fact that he had caught sight of her. As it was, she had the hardest time standing her ground as he advanced, looking older and more worldy-wise than his years should have made him. He looked like a man who had come face-to-face with himself and had held out his hand in acceptance, though clearly without any joy, if the newly added frown lines on his face were testimony. This imagery came and went in her mind as he approached—he was about twenty yards away now. She felt a hint of admiration that he could walk toward her with absolutely no sign of self-consciousness or unease. If it had been she, even with her years of training, she knew she would have begun to look awkward by now, her hands feeling like useless appendages at her sides, her eyes not quite knowing where to look.

Logan, however, was looking directly at her—taking in every detail of her appearance, absorbing her—before he would have to greet her. Was he practicing salutations as she was now doing like mad? She strongly doubted it.

He walked loosely, every muscle relaxed. His worn but scrupulously clean denims fitted like a loving skin over lean hips and muscled thighs. Uniform working gear. No special pains, no scraped-raw look on his hollow cheeks, no dab of hair cream on his clean and healthy ash-brown hair. Still that teak color to his skin. Long days in the sun and a hint of something else—something that made her think a few drops of Indian blood drummed through his veins. Square-jawed, rugged, good-looking, in the inestimable way of the West. She thought he'd make a good model for the Marlboro people.

He came to a standstill a few feet away and had to cock his head to look at her, for the brim of her hat shaded her eyes from him.

"Liz'beth? I know that's you hiding under there."

She lifted her chin immediately, her eyes glinting now as they met his. "Hiding? Why on earth?" she returned flatly.

"That's right. You're still the most beautiful creature on earth, aren't you?" he returned, his voice husky and low.

Hopeless warmth was trying to flood over her, but she held it at bay with an effort. "You're looking good, as well, Logan," she returned with cool politeness. "Unrefined, but good."

He bowed to her a little. "Then you noticed my new shirt?"

"Pink is a difficult color to miss," she returned, refusing to acknowledge the half-hidden smile playing about his lips. She was also refusing to acknowledge that such a feminine color looked absolutely devastating when combined with his raw masculinity. She doubted if he knew that and hoped he didn't.

"I remembered that you once told me you thought dusky pink looked sexy on a man. So I thought I'd give it a whirl."

It was no use, she thought. Besides, this smiling, foxy man was not Logan. The Logans of the world did not wear pink.

"I was hoping to get away with a hello kiss, but you look so perfectly delicious that I'd be bound to muss you up too much."

It simply didn't pay to dwell on every golden sound that passed his lips, particularly when *she* was presently tongue-tied. She looked toward the luggage racks for inspiration.

"It's all taken care of," Logan said, stepping closer and extending his arm. Her fingertips barely alighted.

"How did you know which were mine?" she returned, falling into step with him through the milling throngs of people.

He looked down at her and lifted his brow. "Simple. I just picked the fanciest and most expensive luggage there."

"Was it blue?" she asked faintly, hoping there'd been no mistake.

"A perfect match," he said, meeting her eyes.

Outside, she saw her luggage stacked up in readiness, a uniformed boy standing guard.

"I'll bring the car around," Logan said, "There are too many pieces to carry," he underlined.

"I believe in being prepared. I had no idea how long I would have to stay."

"I'm personally hoping for the whole summer," he returned easily.

"You're hoping it takes an entire summer for James to get back on his feet?" she responded.

"No. Did I say that? I wish James a speedy return to his former stability."

She gave it up with a sense of hopelessness, which deteriorated into downright confusion when he led her directly to a brand-new, midnight-blue Mercedes.

"Logan? Who owns this car?" she said, as he inserted a key in the door and then opened it wide for her.

"The man who holds the keys, of course," he replied. "I just bought it today—on the way to the airport, in fact."

She tucked her skirts in and then watched him walk around to the driver's side. Logan could certainly afford such a car, she thought. It was just that...

"Did the old one break down?" she asked, with an attempt at humor.

He shook his head as he started the smoothly humming motor. "No, but the Chrysler had a dinged fender and it was pretty dusty. And the Land Rover didn't seem quite right somehow."

Elizabeth thought it over as they drove around to pick up her luggage. By the time they left the airport behind and were on the open road, she had made up her mind. Logan was still capable of putting her off kilter with a silly, teasing remark; certainly, he would not have bought a brand-new Mercedes simply for the purpose of taxiing her to his home. That would be utterly ridiculous.

On her guard once more, she said, "Should you have left James? And how come you picked me up instead of sending Hank?"

He answered her in order. "Elvira is taking good care of James, who has a terrific hangover this morning, I might add. And I picked you up because I wanted to, and Hank was needed in the cookhouse. We had a fire there this morning," he went on, "which added nicely to the general confusion. Ben Travers, the cook, burned his hands pretty badly trying to put the grease-fire out. I took him to the hospital here, while Hank and the boys cleaned up the mess in the cookhouse. Then I had a few hours to kill, and I shopped for this," he finished, tapping the wheel.

"In other words, you had to come into Calgary, anyway?"

"I knew you would pick that up. I said I wanted to."

She shrugged as if it made no difference whatever.

"I saw you on television a few nights back," he told her. "In one of those makeup commercials?"

Logan had become a good deal more talkative, she thought. She remembered a predominately silent man listening to the forced gaiety of her conversation. She liked this relaxed and easygoing Logan much better. Of course, they were more on an equal footing now, too. She thought that might have something to do with this subtle change in him.

"How did you like the commercial?" she asked, in reply to his comment.

"I liked it," he said quietly.

Elizabeth looked out her side window. "You came face-to-face with the Rawley Girl a short while ago, and you didn't seem too impressed."

"I was trying to get my breath back. I'd felt as if someone had kicked me in the stomach."

Refusing to admit that he had touched her, she said, "That sounds beautifully rehearsed."

He frowned a little. "You've changed, Liz'beth."

"Obviously."

"I wasn't referring to looks. You were always beautiful— in a more natural way, perhaps." He shrugged. "I was referring to your manner."

"Oh? Did you think I would kiss you like an old friend?"

"No. But then I have no wish to be an old friend of yours."

That hurt, and she felt her eyes prick a little as she continued to keep her face turned from him. "Ditto, I'm sure," she said in a bored tone. "Besides, I'm only out here on account of my father. Is he really as broken as you say?"

"Maybe I exaggerated a little bit," he said, hesitating a moment.

She turned swiftly to face him. "What do you mean?"

The planes of his face took on that hard and immobile look she remembered so well. "Only that it's likely he won't remember much of last night. That gun business, for instance. I wouldn't even mention it to him if I were you."

"Oh. In other words, he's more himself today?"

Logan nodded slowly. "I talked to him about a Gamblers Anonymous organization that apparently holds meetings here in Calgary. That's another thing I was doing this morning, checking up on its whereabouts. James felt desperate enough to agree to it right away when I brought up the subject, so I think I can safely say he's feeling a little more hopeful about things right about now. Hung over, but hopeful."

Elizabeth was looking intrigued. "Gamblers Anonymous? Is that anything like Alcoholics Anonymous?"

Logan nodded. "Very much the same setup. A support group listening to one another and helping one another. As long as an individual really wants to quit and admits to himself that he has a sickness he may not be able to control on his own, it works. As of last night, James admitted it was a sickness—so all the criteria are there. In the future, if he comes under one of his 'spells' as he calls them, help is but a phone call away."

"That sounds wonderful, Logan," Elizabeth said, feeling that here at last was a real solution for her parents.

"Well, it isn't a fait accompli just yet...but, as I told you on the phone, I think James can really beat this thing."

She brought her knees up onto the seat space between them, feeling much more kindly disposed to the man at her side. The scenery, too, was having its effect. They had left the greater city behind, and were now approaching wide-open country—the rolling terrain of prairie land—and in the far distance, the snowy peaks of the mountains beckoned, bringing them closer to the Kananaskis Valley and the Opal L ranch. Pasqueflowers sprinkled themselves in multitudinous array over the landscape as the Mercedes, accelerating, began to eat up the miles.

"Perhaps I'm not needed out here, after all," she said conversationally, beginning to feel the intimacy of the confined space in the luxurious automobile. She removed her hat and placed it on the back seat, allowing the breeze from her partially opened window to gently tease the waves of her hair.

Logan's eyes remained off the road for a little longer than was safe.

"I mean. . ." she went on, her own eyes on the road, "You and James seem to have everything well in hand."

The car careered a little, but Logan swiftly straightened the wheels. "You're needed," he said firmly, after a moment of concentration on his driving.

"Maybe. But what can I do, really? Apart from lending him money, that is. Pat him on the head and say, 'It's all right, James. Mother doesn't really have to know'?"

"Maybe she doesn't," Logan suggested.

Elizabeth regarded him. "Do you really think that would be fair to her?"

"Do you think it's fair to both of them to keep them apart indefinitely? Nothing in this life is certain, is it? Except, now and again, the kind of lasting love a man and a woman can share. James and your mother seem to have that, and I just think it's a damn shame that one game of poker might keep them apart."

Elizabeth sighed. "If you knew what my mother went through as a result of James's gambling, you'd understand why she ought to be told. There shouldn't even be a possibility of her ever having to take a back seat to James's habit again."

"You know what James told me last night? Think about this a moment, Liz'beth, and tell me what the source of James's fever might be. You believe Catherine takes a back seat?" Logan shook his head. "I don't and here's why. James said that he had to shoot for the moon precisely because Catherine was coming back to him. He said that he knew it was going to be his night, when he kept getting dealt hearts. Hearts for his woman...so he could support her in the style she deserved, and the style she was born to." He glanced her way. "I think James has been trying to do this from the day he succeeded in carrying her away from Dragon Manor, expressly against your grandmother's wishes. What was he in those days? A merchant seaman?"

Elizabeth nodded, a frown appearing on her brow as she thought this through. "You're saying James gambles on account of Mother."

"That has to be how it started, at least—way back then. And didn't he settle down a lot in that regard after the divorce? These past six years, at any rate. A game now and again, sure—I even sat in on a few with him, and he dazzled me. He was in peak form, Liz'beth, because at that time, he wasn't afraid to lose. He wasn't compulsive, either. He knew when to quit."

"So the compulsiveness only comes into it when Mother's in the picture?"

Logan nodded. "I think so, yes."

"But that just makes it worse! Don't you see? How will it ever be possible for them to be together if that's the case?"

"Through understanding the reasons. Hell, I'm no psychiatrist, but I think one would tell you that James has always felt inadequate where Catherine is concerned. Not on a conscious level, because he's too dynamic a man to admit something like that to himself. He was poor and proud of it, he'll tell you—just ask him—but that didn't stop him from looking for the winning game, did it? He wanted the spoils for Catherine. And to spite that old dragon who told him that he wasn't fit to wipe her feet."

"Grandmother said that to James?"

"So he tells me."

"Mother doesn't care that much about material things."

"Tell that to James. Over and over again. Maybe it will sink in."

They drove on in silence for a while, Elizabeth totally absorbed in digesting this new food for thought.

After a time, Logan said, "In a way I understand exactly how James feels."

Elizabeth looked at him. "How do you mean?"

"Oh, you know. A man can wish for the moon, when he knows that what he really ought to do is keep his feet firmly planted on the ground. Saves a lot of trouble in the long run."

Elizabeth frowned. "I don't think I understand. Besides, James didn't wish for the moon where my mother was concerned. He reached out and tried to grab at it with both hands. Twice. So how does that apply? To you, I mean..." she trailed off, looking puzzled.

Logan had begun to shake his head slowly, a slight smile softening the hard curve of his lips. "Damned if I know, come to think of it. I must shake James's hand one of these days. He's got more guts than I do—I'll give him that."

"Have I missed something here?"

"Light me a cigarette, will you? They're in the glove box."

"Marlboros, no doubt," she said in slight criticism, moving to do as he asked.

His smile broadened. "Lecture me, Liz—I wouldn't mind."

They weren't Marlboros but unfiltered Players, which she considered just as bad.

Obligingly, she said, "These will kill you, Logan. When was the last time you had a lung X ray? And don't you know that that particular tough cowboy image is passé?"

He was chuckling as she passed him the cigarette with delicate fingers. She had been careful not to inhale.

"I really am planning on quitting one of these days," he said, placing the cigarette between his lips. "But make it easy for me, Liz'beth."

"How?"

"Tell me you'd never kiss a man who was a smoker."

She suddenly realized she was enjoying herself—enjoying Logan's company—too much. Also, her skirt had ridden up, exposing a silken expanse of her thighs, and Logan seemed to be paying particular attention to that fact, looking down frequently. She straightened herself and faced the road. "For the right man," she said, with emphasis, "I might even take it up. Who knows?"

"In other words, I can smoke myself to death, for all you care?"

She shrugged, "It's your health, not mine."

"Thanks for that. I guess I'll just switch to filters, then."

"Suit yourself."

"On all fronts?"

"Once again you have lost me."

"And yet, you consider yourself a very with-it person, don't you?"

She frowned in real impatience now. "Why all the riddles, Logan? And, no, I don't profess to know what you are talking about half the time. When I knew you last you hardly talked at all, in fact."

"When you knew me last I was making the supreme sacrifice. And that can tie up a man's speech pretty much."

"I don't even pretend to know what you're talking about," she said, not wanting to think about what he was saying. It was too easy to jump to the wrong conclusion where Logan was concerned.

"You were the most tempting forbidden fruit ever offered to a man," he said softly in that tone of voice that warned her to swiftly change the conversation.

Putting a hand to the low neckline of her dress, she said, "How much farther now?"

He glanced at her. "Oh, we've got a long way to go yet, Liz'beth."

"You really enjoy these double entendres don't you, Logan? You haven't changed a bit."

"No? What was it last time we were alone? Something about feeling relatively undampened?"

She stared full at him, not in the least expecting him to have had such a clear memory of that pathetic little scene. "You didn't use to use such big words in those days" was all she could manage.

"I guess I wasn't too sure of myself, at that."

"I'd like very much not to discuss this."

"I'd like very much to apologize, Elizabeth—for being a flat-footed brute who really didn't know how to handle the situation."

She did not know what to say or where to look or what to think. Why was he even bringing all this up? It was humiliating—and totally unnecessary. She wanted to forget that entire episode.

"Don't trouble yourself, Logan. I'm a big girl now and past gaffes mean very little to me. I'm surprised that you've even remembered it, to tell you the truth. Lord knows, I'd almost forgotten all about it until you brought it up." She managed a laugh. "I was pretty pathetic, wasn't I? Young girl flipping out over Marlboro Man. I was model-conscious, even then." She looked at him. "You're a sexy-looking man, Logan. Did you know? Your machismo is well in place."

"You don't say," he said flatly.

"Indubitably. You could still set a young girl's heart to fluttering."

"But I'm all washed up with the over-twenty-one set, is that it?"

It was something to know that she could actually get under Logan's skin this way; she could not have pulled it off in the past. His expression, etched in stone, however, warned her to leave well enough alone. The trouble was, her tongue wouldn't listen.

"Oh, well, I'm sure there's a milkmaid or two hereabouts that would give you the eye."

"A milkmaid."

"Uh-huh."

"Sure you don't mean a squaw or two?" he asked softly.

A flippant retort was right there on her lips, but she bit it back just in time. She cast a glance at him. "Why not?" she answered carefully, instead. "Indian women have been known to throw their pennies in the wrong basket, too."

She must have handled it right, for he simply answered, "Why the wrong basket?"

"You're hardly the marrying kind, are you?" she stated.

He was frowning now. "Last I looked, I was as monogamous as the next man. I'm not quite sure where you're coming from, Liz'beth."

"Look how long Kate waited for you to make some kind of commitment. Does she still come around?"

"Yes, because she's still my friend," he finished simply.

"That's all?" she asked, with a delicately arched brow. "After all these years? Poor Kate."

"Leave Kate out of the conversation, okay? You were doing pretty well without her."

"You still don't like to discuss her with me, do you? I guess some things never change."

"Like your inability to change an irrelevant subject."

She shrugged in an unconcerned way, but saw that his mood had subtly changed. The softness in his manner had gone flying out the window along with his half-smoked cigarette. *Good*, she thought. *I don't need your indulgence.*

"You could start a brush fire that way," she snapped.

"I pinched it out first," he returned just as abruptly.

Feeling quite safe from his presence, his riddles and his double entendres, Elizabeth accepted his mood with a certain amount of equanimity. She turned away from him and watched the scenery silently for many miles, feeling the embrace of the approaching mountains.

4

LOGAN AT LAST MADE A TURN, leaving the highway to turn onto a secondary road that led into steadily rising foothills. It was at the crest of one of these that the Opal L finally came into view. Its huge, sprawling borders were visibly marked by mountains and the natural boundary of a river tributary.

"You must feel like a king," she murmured, forgetting their contretemps as she enjoyed this forgotten view of his land.

He didn't respond, but she could see he was now looking at it through her eyes and seeing the majesty of it.

"A baron, at any rate," he admitted with only a little mockery. "Like my father before me. So I can't take too much credit, can I?"

Elizabeth felt he was being modest. In spite of the economy of the times and his youthful takeover on his father's death, he had managed to hang on to all of this, when so many other cattle barons had been forced to sell off huge chunks of their land, decreasing their output accordingly.

"Stop a minute," she asked him.

He obligingly brought the vehicle to a halt, turning in his seat to look at her when the ignition was off. "What do you see?" he asked her, taking note of the expression on her face.

What she saw was land spread out in all directions. She was looking at hills and valleys and lakes and streams and a hushed setting in the shadow of the Rockies. She was seeing wide open spaces and the romantic vision of a lone cowboy silhouetted against an evening sky, despite the fact that it was presently high noon. She felt that she had stepped out of time into a land and a way of life that was fast disappearing. She wanted to hold on to it for as long as she could.

"Do you realize this is unique?" she said, trying to put her feelings into words. She saw dots of cattle grazing on an open range. "Those cattle, for instance," she pointed out. "Spread out over thousands of acres. How many breeders today can still use the old methods of ranging cattle? What could you compare this to today?"

"The King Ranch in Texas is a close comparison, I guess," he said, his eyes still on her.

"The famed King Ranch," she agreed. "Logan, I get such a strange feeling looking at all this."

"Share it with me, Liz'beth." His voice was an octave lower.

She parted her lips, then shook her head as she was about to speak. "I can't," she said, placing her hand on her heart. "I don't know how to put it into words."

His eyes had been drawn to her breasts, and this was the first thing she noticed when she turned to look at him. The second thing, when his eyes made contact with hers, was the darkened depths she was looking into. From safe sanity to drowning confusion could take only an instant, she realized, before all thought broke down completely.

The dark, burning flames in his eyes drew nearer, and then his mouth hovered over hers. "You shouldn't have shown me this other side of you," he murmured, beginning to taste her more fully now. "I was all right until your eyes began to shine..."

No other words were possible in the ensuing urgency of the kiss. Elizabeth's mouth opened for him before she could even think to prevent it, and then she was being subjected to passion so all-consuming that it communicated itself to her like a brush fire. She had no notion that Logan would ever kiss her like this—indeed, it was the first time his lips had ever touched hers. She remembered how tentatively she had approached the corner of his mouth those growing years ago, and the ecstasy she had felt when he did not draw away. If he had kissed her like this then, she would have fainted at his feet.

His touch was in her hair and along the length of her arm, then settled on the fullness of a soft breast. She felt an electric shock that angled downward, and then she was breathing with an intensity to match his as his tongue became a sensual, seeking blade.

This absolutely cannot be happening, she told herself, trying desperately hard to break his emotional hold on her. It was like peeking under the lid of a pot, only to have the contents immediately boil over. What she had to do, before she lost all control of herself and of the situation entirely, was safely get the lid back on the pot.

With a great effort, she managed to free her mouth then hissed breathlessly, "Stop this, Logan."

"You don't want me to stop," he said huskily against her ear, "Not after kissing me back like that."

She felt his warm breath filling all the hollows there, and it was almost her undoing.

"Yes, I do," she said raggedly, thankful that he had at least removed his hand from her breast. To ensure her safe return to rationality, she added, "I'm used to more *finesse*, Logan."

He drew away to the extent that she felt quite bereft.

"You really know how to put a man in his place, don't you?" he said, his voice and his expression giving her no indication of emotional upheaval within. By the time he made his next comment, however, it was worse, for his eyes had gone quite dead. "I guess you bring out the ancestral savage in me, Liz'beth." He shrugged philosophically, as if the entire incident was of no significance.

She itched to slap that bland and uncaring look off his face, but knew she wouldn't dare. Logan had become an entirely new entity to her—fathoms deep—and she didn't want to fall in over her head.

She was relieved when he started the engine and moved into forward gear. They skirted the rise and began their descent into a tree-dotted basin, where in the distance she saw the main buildings huddled together in a group. Drawing nearer, Elizabeth was able to make out the large structure of the house, and then the long, low roofs of the bunkhouses off to the left. To the right were the barns and stables and paddocks, and a huge corral fronted all the buildings, its white wood fencing looking like chalk lines on the green and sienna surface of the landscape.

As they continued to descend, the Opal Mountain peaks seemed to rise ever higher, blocking out the western sky and causing a dizzying sensation to sweep over her. She looked up at the snow-shrouded summits and imagined how it must feel to stand so far above the earth and look down upon the anthills of human life—for that sense of their majesty was unmistakable.

A queasy stomach and a throbbing in her temples reminded her she was in no shape for such imagery, however regardless of how effective it was in keeping her mind off what had so recently occurred between Logan and herself. Charles, too, was insinuating himself into her mind, making her realize that from the moment of her meeting with Logan she had forgotten his entire existence.

She put a hand to her brow and rubbed, wishing that she had not agreed to stay at Logan's home and wondering why it was necessary, anyway. According to Logan, James had recovered somewhat from his deep depression of the evening before. Perhaps she and James would be able to—

"Headache?" Logan inquired quietly, interrupting her train of thought.

She nodded, but ceased her soothing action against her brow as though she'd been caught in a secret act. "I...I'm not too good with flying, I'm afraid, so I didn't dare eat anything this morning, and—"

"Why didn't you say so?" he asked, frowning. "I assumed you had eaten on the plane, or I would have taken you somewhere for a bite to eat before setting off."

"It doesn't matter. I'm sure we'll be arriving for lunch, won't we?"

He nodded, but the hardness in his expression did not relax. He drove down a long winding drive, braking in front of the sprawling yet graceful two-story house with a wide veranda.

A collie, which had been stretched out on the front step, basking in the sun, got stiffly to his feet and began to wag his tail in greeting.

Elizabeth opened her door before Logan quite made it around to her side and stood up with a grateful stretch.

"I trust you remember Tornado," he said, as the dog ambled happily toward them.

Elizabeth stooped down to scratch the sleek, sloping head. "How are you, old fella?" she murmured, trying to figure out his age.

"He certainly remembers you," Logan said, watching her with the dog. "Careful he doesn't jump up on that fancy dress of yours."

Elizabeth was taking due care but wished that she had dressed more appropriately for this particular moment. It was ridiculous, she told herself, to feel all choked up simply because an arthritic old dog was gazing up at her with worshipful eyes—a look he reserved for long-lost friends.

In a curious way this welcoming dog seemed to recapture the feelings that had welled up in her when they had arrived at the crest of Logan's land—the feelings she had not been able to put a name to...and on a deeper level, had not wanted to.

"Miz Liz! Miz Liz!" called a wizened old figure, gingerly rounding the house just as Logan was about to escort her up the steps with several pieces of her luggage.

Elizabeth set down a light case to return Hank's wave of welcome, keeping her makeup case in her left hand. Logan, overly burdened with the rest as he was, merely looked in the ranch hand's direction.

"Hank," Elizabeth said, when the old fellow had drawn near. "You haven't changed a bit."

Hank's eyes were wide in appraisal and admiration as he stood at the bottom of the steps, his close-up view of her, in fact, rendering him tongue-tied.

Logan's lips curved dryly. "Another one bites the dust," he said quietly, for her ears alone.

"Aren't you going to speak to me, Hank?" Elizabeth said, ignoring Logan.

Hank swiftly removed his beat-up hat. "I...maybe I'd better come around when I've cleaned up some, first, Miz Liz...I mean Ms. Jackson," he said, flushing and looking uncomfortable.

Elizabeth hid her regrets over her rather flamboyant appearance, saying, "Liz will do just fine, Hank, as it always has. And why would you feel you'd need to get cleaned up just for my arrival? I plan on getting my jeans on just as soon as I'm able."

None of which seemed to put Hank at his ease as he stood there shuffling his feet. He flashed a semitoothless grin, however, as he began to back off. Shaking his head, he said, "I don't think that's quite gonna do it, Miz Liz. I shore don't. These eyes ain't never seen a picture like you, an' that's the truth. So most likely you're gonna be seeing me peerin' around at you, trying not to be too pesky-like. But if it should get on your nerves, you just say, 'Scat, varmint,' and I'll be gone just as fast as these bow legs will take me."

Elizabeth, feeling uncomfortable, glanced at Logan, who was trying to control a slight twitching in his lips.

"Oh, boss?" Hank said, his head suddenly appearing atop a veranda rail.

"Yeah, Hank."

"I was meaning to ask you about Ben. His hands gonna be all right?"

Logan nodded. "Second-degree in a few areas. He should be back to work in a few weeks."

"Then I'm gonna be doin' the cooking for a spell?"

"'Fraid so, Hank."

Hank frowned, bobbed and was gone again.

"The old relic," Logan said fondly, shouldering open the screen door for Elizabeth to pass through. "He still thinks cooking is 'sissy work' and feels he ought to be out bronco bustin' and such. Hey! Out!" he said to the dog, who was trying to slink through unnoticed, close to Elizabeth's high heels. "What have you done to that dog, Liz'beth! He's slathering over you even worse than Hank."

Before Elizabeth could come up with a response, a small black-haired woman crossed the foyer, rubbing her hands on a polka-dotted apron. Her dark eyes passed over Elizabeth as she frowned at Logan. "Why isn't Cade helping with that?" she said, indicating the luggage in their hands. "He was around here a few minutes ago."

"Didn't see him," Logan said simply, setting the luggage down and taking Elizabeth's cases from her hands. "Go and see if you can round him up, will you, Elvira? He can have the honor of the trip up the stairs."

Elvira nodded and then held out a still floury hand to Elizabeth. "Sorry, Miss Jackson, that it is not your father greeting you," she said, her words clipped. "But he is in the shower—" she glanced at Logan "—trying to unredden his eyes for his daughter's arrival."

Logan acknowledged that with a flat smile, while Elizabeth shooked the proffered hand.

"That's all right, Elvira," she said. "Actually, I was hoping to freshen up myself before speaking to him." Elvira's discomfiture at Elizabeth's appearance had been the last straw,

in Elizabeth's estimation. No matter that such perfect care
had been taken in her appearance in order to better arm herself against her memories of Logan, the time had come for
more casual dress. She had no wish to make everyone she met
feel at a disadvantage. Or even worse, make them think that
she considered herself too good for them, an impression she
had gleaned from the look in Elvira's eyes.

As Logan guided her across the freshly waxed wooden
floor to the base of the stairs, she thought in annoyance that
she had outfitted herself as if she were going to be doing one
photo session after another—none of them against a backdrop of hay bales. Unless one considered two chic cowgirl
outfits imported from Spain, no less, she had very little to
wear around the ranch. Thank goodness for her two pairs of
jeans; even though they were in cranberry and ocher colors,
they were better than nothing.

Elvira went off in search of her son, Cade, while Elizabeth
preceded Logan up the stairs, looking at the beautiful Indian
tapestry that covered the facing wall of the landing. She removed her hat once again as she drew level with the intricate
hanging; and then she turned to look down at Logan, a questioning comment on her lips. She did not recall the tapestry
being there before on any of her previous visits.

But Logan was still near the base of the steps. He had forgotten where he was as he watched her ascent, the long, slim
legs drawing his eyes to the curve of her hips as she mounted
each stair. She knew this was so when she met his gaze, for
he was now admiring the view from his very advantageous
position. Pressing her skirt against her thighs, she frowned
at him.

"Your legs go on forever—did you know that?" he murmured, lifting his eyes to her face.

A warmth stole over her and left her feeling breathless. She
counteracted it by deepening her frown. "Are you quite

through playing the Peeping Tom now?" she asked him coldly.

"All done," he said, beginning to move slowly up the stairs to her.

Elizabeth felt like backing against the wall, but instead moved quickly up the remaining stairs. In the upstairs hall, she waited for him to draw abreast of her, since she did not know where her room would be.

"This way," he directed, and she was sure his soft brushing against her as he moved around her was no accident.

She followed, keeping a wary eye on the back of his head then nearly bumping into him when he stopped at the second door to the right of the hallway, facing the back of the house.

He showed her into a corner room, saying, "James's is the door at the far end of the hall."

"And where is yours?" she asked, looking around the room. The delicate floral motif of the wallpaper was repeated on the bedspread and the softly billowing curtains, giving the heavy oak furniture a light and graceful touch. It was a large room—almost of master-bedroom proportions —and she saw a door leading into what was obviously an ensuite bathroom.

"Close by," Logan said noncommittally. "This isn't exactly the Waldorf-Astoria, you know."

"But it's very nice," she said, meaning it, and walked into the room. "Is that bed on a pedestal?" she asked, observing the raised and canopied structure.

"It is. This was my mother's room."

"Oh?" she said with interest. Logan had never spoken about his mother to her before. She gave herself a reminder to ask him about her someday. "And did your father enjoy placing her on a pedestal?"

Logan gave her a caustic look. "Don't get me started. My old man wasn't the pedestal-placing type. Not that my mother would have wanted it, anyway. As far as I can remember, the bed just came with the house. It's probably close to a century old."

Elizabeth smoothed her fingers lightly over the handcarved bedpost, enjoying the look of the old polished wood. "I hope you realize what a treasure you have in Elvira," she said, when absolutely no dust came away on her fingers. She glanced at Logan when he didn't respond and saw that his features had taken on that familiar stony look.

"Elvira isn't a treasure," he told her, letting her know he didn't care for the term. "She's a relative of mine. Or didn't you know that, Liz'beth?"

She hadn't, and she supposed a bit of her surprise showed, though not for the reasons Logan was obviously thinking.

To forestall any further comment, which Elizabeth was reasonably assured was forthcoming, she said, "Honestly, Logan, I don't know why you have to make such a point of it. So Elvira's a distant relative of yours. So what? I think it's nice that you have some semblance of family around you. I'd always thought of you as entirely on your own."

"Elvira's my cousin," he told her. "Not so distant."

"Then your grandparent was..."

"A descendant of the Assiniboine tribe. And it was our grandmother."

"How proud you must be," she said, meeting his gaze levelly.

His look became derisive. "Come off it, Elizabeth. Who do you think you're trying to kid?"

"No one," she said firmly. "Because I've always thought of the Indian Heritage as the most culturally beautiful of them all. As far as I'm concerned, we're the intruders."

"Walk with me through an Indian reserve one of these days...and your romantic vision might drop a notch or two."

"I'm aware that we've robbed them blind of their land and of most of their proud spirit. If I walked through a reserve I would feel ashamed of my people, Logan, not yours."

"Well-chosen words, Elizabeth, but I still don't buy it. Not entirely. How would you feel about marrying a half-breed, for instance? Just as a case in point, you understand. You'd have to bear in mind that one or two of your children would be apt to come in for some ostracizing from their play-mates—told to go back to the reserve where they belong."

"I may or may not be strong enough for that aspect of it. I really don't know. If I couldn't bring my children up in a less bigoted atmosphere, I suppose I would choose not to have any because that would hurt me too much. People can really be disgusting sometimes, can't they, Logan?" The last was said with a look of pain in her eyes for those imagined children.

Logan was looking pained himself, but for a much different reason. "Why do you keep doing this to me?" he said. "Just when I think I've got you all figured out, and I'm planning nefarious ways of dealing with my raw need, you throw me a curve ball." He shook his head as he walked to the door. "Now I've got to rework my strategy, and I think the one to help me out on that is James. I'll go see if his eyes are less bloodshot, and if he's got the courage yet to come out and face you—his too-beautiful daughter who can look so cold and haughty that you wish a wart would grow on her nose and then suddenly makes you wish that you really were Prince Charming."

As Logan went away muttering, Elizabeth sat down on the bed weakly, wondering what on earth all that was about. She touched her finger to the tip of her nose and then looked up startled when a young Indian man appeared in her doorway, heavily burdened with her blue leather luggage.

"Excuse me," he said politely. "I was told to bring this up here."

Elizabeth sprang up and came forward, realizing that Cade had been but a boy of fourteen when she'd last seen him. He obviously didn't recognize her.

She took two of her cases from him and then thanked him when he deposited the rest near her bed. Grateful for his retreat, since he, too, had begun to stare, Elizabeth swiftly closed and locked her door and began peeling off her clothes as she walked toward the bathroom, with the full intention of making herself as plain looking as possible.

Standing in bra and panties, she washed the Rawley foundation off her face, along with the blusher, mascara, eyeliner and shadow. When she was through, her face shone with the kiss of nature. Diminishing the shine just a bit with a dab or two of powder, she contented herself by simply applying lip gloss in a very pale, muted shade. She then rummaged through her case for an elastic band, bringing her hair back into a simple ponytail. She stared at the effect and hated it, knowing this just wasn't her. Nature, she decided, intended ponytails to be worn on horses.

Still...it was better than having people stare at her all the time—thinking her unapproachable, which definitely seemed to be the case in this neck of the woods. If she didn't look at herself, this new image wouldn't bother her too much.

She was about to leave the bathroom to "put on some duds" when she noticed a connecting door just to the right of the curtained tub. It opened freely, and she then was looking upon a rather starkly appointed room, neat and tidy enough to give no clue to its occupant—except for one thing. Logan was lying on his back on the bed, his booted feet crossed and his elbows bent at right angles to his head. His eyes, however, were drifting directly over her scantily clad form.

She placed her hands on naked hips, standing her ground.

"Just what do you think you're doing?" she asked.

"Resting," he said. "And looking at the view."

"I thought you were going to talk to James," she countered as if that were the main point.

"I knocked and he replied that he'd be down in a minute, and to have the chow on because he was starved. You might say he kind of knocked the wind out of my romantic sails."

"Romantic," she muttered, as if she had never heard the word before. "Is romance what you had in mind when you placed me in the room connecting with yours?'

"In a manner of speaking, yes." He sat up on the bed and frowned. "What have you done to your hair?"

She was surprised his eyes had managed to find that particular feature. "Don't trouble yourself about it—I only pulled it back for washing."

"Good thing."

"Are there locks on these doors?"

"Nope."

"Then I want another room."

"Sorry—all out."

"I don't believe that."

"Come over here, Liz'beth."

"Madman."

His eyes fell to her breasts. "There was a time when you would have come freely," he murmured.

"Obviously you aren't all bound up in my age now, are you, Logan? But haven't you noticed? I'm a far cry from that girl you used to know. So don't consider me fair game."

"I don't."

"Get one thing straight, Logan. I came here only for the purpose of helping my parents, and because you offered to help, as well."

"I meant that."

"Then I would like you to stop this."

"Stop what?"

"These sexual plans you have where you and I are concerned. They aren't going to pan out, no matter what form of strategy you come up with. I'm used to dealing with men on the make, Logan."

"And that's what you think I am?" He swung his legs off the bed and got to his feet. "But I can hardly deny it when you're presently making my mouth water, can I? Do you usually talk to men while you're standing around in those wisps that pass for underwear? I can't think straight, let alone answer your questions," he said, slowly approaching her. "I'm just not that blasé, Elizabeth."

"You stay where you are," Elizabeth said, backing up a step as she kept hold of the knob of the door. "Goodness, Logan—"

"Has nothing to do with it," he said, grabbing the door just as she was about to shut it.

She pulled fruitlessly and then looked up at him furiously. "I don't buy this! There are women on the public beaches who wear less than I've got on now!"

"They aren't you," he murmured, his other hand grasping her wrist now. "Besides, I've never had time for the beach..."

"Don't," she said, when his other hand released the door and slipped to the back of her bare waist. He brought her to him, despite the fact she was still holding on to the knob.

"Logan," she warned, her senses beginning to swim as she looked up at him. "I...don't want this..."

"Then do it for me, Liz'beth," he breathed against her mouth. "Do it for all the years I've waited for you...."

Hungrily his mouth began to move on hers, and as before, his need communicated itself to her in such a way that she felt anchorless, felt the world shifting as his arms embraced her possessively, fitting her slender, half-naked form against the roughness of his clothing while his hand smoothed her softness from shoulder to thigh.

Her mouth began to feel ravished, her skin raw where his belt buckle was cutting into her; and when he swung her up in his arms, she took the opportunity to gasp for breath, saying protestingly, "Logan, Logan. Slow down. You...hurt me."

He looked down into her face, his chest heaving and his own breathing tortured. She saw the effort he made to quiet himself, and then he was carrying her to the bed, sinking to a sitting position, cradling her on his lap.

"Elizabeth," he said hoarsely, his hands and his lips more gentle on her now. "This isn't me. Do you understand what I'm saying? I don't move in on women like this. I'm no Casanova, but I'm no charging bull, either. At least not normally. You do this to me."

Her hand smoothed his sun-bronzed cheek, and then her fingers traced the squareness of his jaw, the tip of one of them finding the slight indentation just under his bottom lip.

"I think you have a dimple," she murmured.

"Liz'beth, have you been listening to me?"

A soft smile touched her lips. "Yes. Sometimes you talk too much, Logan."

A slight curve came to his own lips. "I just can't please you, can I? And here I was trying to employ a little *finesse*."

"Finesse isn't all it's cracked up to be."

"Feisty, aren't you?" he murmured, a tender and amused light in his eyes as his gaze roamed her face.

Elizabeth could feel a heavy constriction in her throat, formed by the look in those eyes. She had never supposed Logan would look at her this way. Danger signals warned, but she wanted to ignore them for just a little while. This was a Logan that her eyes had never seen before—and they were devouring him hungrily, capturing his every nuance of expression, his every word.

God help me, she thought. *I could love him again so easily.*

Inevitably, as she knew they would, his eyes fell to the creamy swell of her breasts above her lace bra, and tenderness gave way to sensuality.

"You look good enough to eat." His voice was so low that she could hardly catch the words. She sensed the effort he was making to hold back, to make no overt moves because of her lack of clothing. She was here, in his room, on his lap, in her underwear, a scant half an hour after entering his home. He would be a fool to rush after gaining so much.

And why had she stood there letting him look at her after she had discovered he was in this room? A woman only did that if she wanted to be made love to.

Elizabeth suddenly felt sick and disgusted with herself. Six years' distance had apparently done her little good where Logan was concerned. She still wanted him and probably always would. She, who had somehow managed to forget what passion was all about. What a bad joke on her this was bound to become.

She looked at Logan and tried to think of a way to nip this in the bud . If he just wouldn't look at her in that tender, sexy way she could probably withstand the test—she could probably keep her distance. What was the very best way to dampen a man's desire *and* gain his dislike? The latter should rightly have been accomplished by now, for her behavior was certainly not her best when she was in his company, but apparently he had decided to overlook a lot.

"Don't worry," he murmured, seeing a hint of distress in her face. "I want to devour you whole...but I can enjoy this, too. Just holding you, looking at you, thinking ahead to what we might share..."

His hand, smoothing her upper arm, moved up to her hair, and now his fingers tugged gently at the elastic band that held its richness from his view.

"Don't do that," she said, jerking her head.

"Did I hurt you?" His look was one of concern.

"No. But I'll fix my own hair, if you don't mind."

He regarded her steadily for a minute. "Will the real Elizabeth Jackson please step forward?" he said.

"She did better than that, and you should count yourself lucky." She shifted and then slipped off his lap quickly. "This little intimate scene is starting to bore me now."

"You don't say." His expression hadn't changed.

"I do say."

"I don't buy this about-face, Elizabeth. And you're forgetting something else."

"Oh? And what would that be?"

"We've known each other since the time you were sixteen. The cold, haughty woman I'm looking at now is not the real you. So you can cut the act."

"It is no act! I happen to dislike you intensely, Logan."

He rose, and she hated the fact that she had to look up at him. With high heels, her five-foot-seven-inch height usually put her on an equal footing with men. Logan, at six three, seemed to tower above her now as she stood in her bare feet, bracing herself in case he decided to make a physical show of his strength.

"I happen to think you're out for some revenge," he returned evenly. "I don't particularly blame you, but try and look at it from my side, Liz'beth. I couldn't see myself being selfish enough to tie you down here—to try and hold you here. Your youth was only a small part of it. Mostly I just knew you didn't belong here."

She didn't know why that last statement hurt her so much, but it did. She stood in front of him, unable to respond, for it was so very necessary to put a clamp on that hurt.

With a soft impatient sound, Logan strode to his closet, opened the door and extracted a robe. He brought it to her saying, "Put that on, Elizabeth. Otherwise I can't be responsible for putting my thoughts into actions." He placed it around her shoulders, and she clutched the edges together as he moved in front of her.

"I still know that," he went on, "and I'll try to keep it in mind if I should ever again get the opportunity to try and se- duce you. Fair warning, Elizabeth," he added softly. "I will try. I wanted you then and I want you now, in spite of the fact that where our two worlds are concerned the twain can never meet."

"How poetic," she said tightly. "But what is all this in aid of? To assure yourself that I won't get any ideas where you're concerned? You don't have to worry! As I said before, I wouldn't have even come here if it weren't for James! So what I would really like—putting your wants aside—is for you to make yourself scarce while I concern myself with the prob- lem at hand! The reason for my presence here!"

He bowed to her, saying, "Your wish is my command, Liz'beth. It always has been."

Feeling as though she were about to explode, she made a swift and stormy exit from the room, slamming the con- necting doors as she went.

Once in her own room, however, the self-defence mecha- nism of her anger drained away, and she sank to the edge of her bed and viewed her inner self with patent disgust.

She pulled the elastic band from her hair, knowing that she would never wear her hair pulled back that plainly again— because Logan didn't like it.

She had been in his company for less than three hours and already she was hooked. She could deny it all she wanted, but while doing so, her body was steadily humming a pagan song.

She tried to conjure up Charles and all the things he stood for, but it wasn't any good. The main reason being that she was having the gravest difficulty bringing his features to her mind's eye.

She knew he was handsome and intelligent and sensitive and decent and good. She knew all that, but at the moment it was a little like learning the multiplication tables by rote. Charles and Elizabeth added up to the perfect couple—and with him she could keep her career and her psyche intact.

Logan and Elizabeth added up to...torture.

She rubbed at her arms and thought about agony and ecstasy and the passionate affair that had been her parents' marriage. She then thought about Logan's chief interest in her, and whether she could accept it for what it was—a sexual urgency six years in the making.

It could all be so simple if only she could forget that freshfaced girl who would have gladly cut out her heart for him...

She stood up, her features contorted. For an instant, all the pain had come rushing back. She had known clearly and absolutely, at that very tender age, that Logan could satisfy all her yearnings. She would have placed herself in his hands without giving such things as a career, a strong self-image or hard-working independence a thought. Such things would have bored her to death in comparison to her feelings for Logan.

How frightening! What danger there! She might as well have been her mother, starry-eyed, running off with James.

A short while later, her touched-up features perfectly composed, Elizabeth made a fast check of herself in the bathroom mirror. Although she had put on the cranberry jeans for practicality's sake, the pink silk, long-sleeved blouse she was wearing could never remotely resemble "duds." Her hair was brushed and fluffed out to its fullest, and there were slim gold hoops in her ears. The delicate heart locket at her throat was actually a tiny case for her contacts, and she found it particularly useful when traveling. On her feet were highheeled sandals that in Toronto would be considered fairly casual—the type to be worn with pants or jeans. But in this setting, Elizabeth knew they branded her as a city slicker;

everyone here wore well-scuffed boots of the Western or moccasin variety.

She left her room feeling self-assured and intact and fairly certain that she would not become too emotional or maudlin on meeting James. That would do neither of them any good. His bedroom door was ajar, indicating that he had made his exit and was likely downstairs waiting for her in Logan's study. This proved to be true.

"It's about time I got another look at that face of yours! It seems I have to get myself into one hell of an unholy mess before you'll condescend to visit me!" James greeted her.

Grateful to him for breaking the ice in this gruff way, Elizabeth smiled as she moved forward to hug him and kiss his cheek, conscious of the need to blink away sudden moisture in her eyes. "James," she said, her voice husky, "for a while there, Logan had me very worried about you. But I see you're back in form, as usual."

Father and daughter drew back to look at each other.

"You're beautiful," they both said in unison, for it was a standard greeting each made to the other whenever they met over the years. Elizabeth laughed as she took hold of his outstretched arm.

"Logan said I'm to do the honors in his absence. Apparently his able body is needed elsewhere for the day."

"He said something about spring roundup," Elizabeth commented nonchalantly as James led her toward the dining room.

James nodded. "It's a busy time around here—not a good time for a neighbor or a friend to be...down on his luck. But Logan came through for me, as usual. He's a good man, Elizabeth."

Elizabeth murmured a response.

"In another couple of days, the herd will all be in and Logan will have more time to spare. Then the two of you can—"

"James," Elizabeth broke in quickly. "I did not come here to spend time with Logan. I came for your benefit."

James patted her arm. "Sure, honey, and I appreciate it. But I don't think there's much you can do for me."

Once again tears clouded her eyes, for she saw how very brave he was being. As he pulled out her chair, she said carefully, "Perhaps not, but I'd like to try, James...and so would Logan. He...he mentioned something about your willingness to try Gamblers Anonymous."

James nodded as he moved into a place beside her. "That I am. Like the old wino, I feel as though I've hit the bottom of the barrel. To think that I could gamble away that kind of money and horse value just before your mother was due to—" He broke off and shook his head, the mellowing rays of the afternoon sun making him suddenly look old to Elizabeth. Old and beaten.

This cannot be James Jackson, she told herself, feeling a lump growing in her throat. James Jackson, in his worst moods, was still the charming riverboat gambler, the devil-may-care rogue who had stolen her mother's heart and then had simply put it into his pocket for safekeeping, patting it from time to time through Elizabeth, just to ensure that it was still there. James Jackson never gave up on anything, least of all on himself.

Elizabeth was suddenly absolutely convinced that James would never gamble again. She had never seen such a desolate look on his face before—not even during the time of her parents' separation.

Fighting back tears, she said, "James, I...strongly feel you can beat this thing. So does Logan."

James nodded. "Better late than never, I guess," he replied.

Even if she could have come up with a response to that, one wasn't possible, for Elvira entered the room, carrying a large tray of assorted cold cuts and salads.

James rose to assist her, while Elizabeth fought to compose her emotions. This will never do, she told herself. If Elvira had not interrupted, she probably would have blurted out something silly and grossly unfair about her mother. Of course her mother had to know about this. There was no way she could advise James not to tell her. Besides, it would do her well to remember that James had always had the ability to play on her emotions—to create a war between the two people who often seemed to reside inside her. Elizabeth's lips became a little dry. Really, she could be torn two ways at the drop of a hat.

With a smile aimed at James and a curt nod in Elizabeth's direction, Elvira left the room. Elizabeth tried to take the snub philosophically, promising herself that from here on in, she would offer to help with the preparation of the meals. She was not a bad cook, actually.

"If Logan were at the table, I don't think Elvira would feel she's being put out so much," Elizabeth commented to James, partly as a means to change the previous subject, and partly because she was feeling a little hurt by Elvira's curtness.

James shrugged and then frowned a little. "She isn't particularly friendly toward you, is she?"

"You noticed. I guess it would have helped if I didn't look like such a glamour girl. Tonight I'll offer my assistance in the kitchen. Maybe I can make her change her mind about me."

James's frown increased. "You're Logan's guest, Elizabeth, just as I am for the present. He wouldn't expect or want you to be doing any kitchen work. And under normal circumstances it wouldn't even enter your head," he finished discerningly.

Elizabeth looked up at him in the process of filling her plate high. "Now, what's that supposed to mean?"

"It means that racism is rearing its ugly head. There's such a thing as overcompensation, you know, Liz. Going out of your way to make sure the other person doesn't think that you harbor any bigotry in your soul? *I* know that isn't you, so what's the problem?"

Elizabeth gave him a stiff smile. "That's very perceptive of you, James. You're right—the racial part of it is definitely not my problem. The problem is, she's Logan's cousin, so I don't feel right about her waiting on me."

James shrugged. "Same difference, if you ask me. Cousin or not, she still works for him."

Elizabeth might have responded if her mouth had not been full of potato salad. She was ravenous, and she noticed that James was digging right in, as well. Obviously he could still eat well in the face of desolation. She tried not to look at it this way, and indeed felt a little guilty about the thought. It was terrible not being able to really trust someone you loved.

"So how's the old dragon?" James asked her after a while, looking as though his spirits had rebounded a bit.

Elizabeth did not decrease her intake, saying instead around a forkful of food, "James, Grandmother really isn't so bad. You just got off on the wrong foot with her."

"You can say that again." For a moment, moroseness seemed to overtake him, but Elizabeth could see him visibly trying to clear it away. "And where did you learn to talk with a mouthful of food like that? Not from her, I'll bet."

Elizabeth set her fork down and swallowed her food carefully, realizing that she had been making a pig of herself while inwardly criticizing James for his appetite. She attempted to explain.

"You have to realize that I've been near starving myself for two years—ever since I got the Rawley Girl spot. I now have the opportunity to stuff myself for two months, at least. So if you think that mere table manners are going to deter me, my dear old duff, you've got another thing coming."

James hid a smile. "Bull, Elizabeth," he said easily. "You always were the type who could eat her own weight in food and not put on a pound. So don't give me that starvation business. No, the way I see it, you're suffering from the same malady I am. The day-after syndrome. How much did you drink on the plane today?"

Elizabeth felt discomfitted. "I had brandy with my coffee, James," she said in a demure manner. "And that's all."

"Yeah?"

"Yeah."

"No tranquilizers? No trusty-dusty Gravol?" he said, eyeing her as he shoved an entire deviled egg into his mouth.

Elizabeth pressed her lips together in an attempt at offended dignity, but then gave it up with soft laughter and blue-eyed sparkle of amusement. "You're right on," she said, picking up her fork with a challenge in her eyes.

"*Gusto*," James said.

"Winner gets the extra deviled egg," Elizabeth pronounced, matching his forkfuls.

"Loser has to eat the banana pickles," James returned, beginning to outdistance her.

Elizabeth chortled gleefully when she gained the lead by helping herself to seconds. "James, James. Do you know how awful this is for the digestion?" she said, though she could hardly speak for laughing.

"This is also bad for the image," James said, a string of coleslaw stuck to his chin. "Shame on you, Elizabeth Claybourne Jackson—what would the world say if it could see you with a glob of Jell-O on your nose?"

Elizabeth crossed her eyes and looked down. "There seems to be a sliver of carrot on it, as well."

"You're good for me, Liz," James said, leaning back and patting his heart rather than his stomach. "Why did you stay away so long? Didn't have anything to do with Logan, did it?"

Feeling that the fun was suddenly over, Elizabeth picked up her napkin and tidied herself. "Why would you think that, James?" she asked a little coolly.

"What else am I supposed to think? You never ostracized me before. Maybe I deserved it, but you never did, Liz. And for that I was always thankful."

"Don't get me choked up, please, Dad." Her tears seemed only a moment away.

"You called me Dad," James said.

She tried to smile. "Did I? Well, Mother is insisting these days."

James's expression remained carefully unchanged. "That's the only reason, then?"

Elizabeth kept her face bright, despite the fact that she was envisioning her father putting a gun to his head. "Of course not," she said. "You're my old dad and I'll address you accordingly."

James's strong, good-looking features contorted a bit. "'Old Dad'?" he said, verbalizing his protest. "On second thought, honey, you can just go on calling me James."

"I thought that would settle it," Elizabeth allowed, trying to study her father objectively. As a young girl, she had seen a movie based on one of Ian Fleming's famous books—Sean Connery had played the lead, of course. Perhaps it had had a lot to do with the fact that the character and her father had shared the same first name, but Elizabeth had decided then and there that "Bondishness" was simply a matter of temperament. It had nothing to do with spy games or intrigue. It was the way both Jameses handled themselves in any situation. To Elizabeth, their sauve self-assurance was identical, and if it weren't for the cobalt-blue eyes, James, at this age and stage, highly resembled the still-handsome actor right down to the receding hairline and the newly formed lines of dissipation in his face. Gambling fever or no, her father was highly attractive to women, and as a result, Elizabeth had often wondered if—

"I take it your mother told you all about our plans," James said, breaking into her thoughts. His expression once again looked pained.

But was it really going to be all right? Elizabeth asked herself, already forgetting her former promise to herself. Could James possibly understand the devastation her mother was going to feel? Did he understand that he was her mother's lifeline and always had been? How could he continue to hurt her like this? And yes, he probably had slept with other women—plenty of times. Her mother, on the other hand—

"Elizabeth? Did you hear me?" James said.

Elizabeth nodded with a bit of a start. "Yes. Yes, Mother told me all about the plans to...get married again."

"And how did you feel about it?" James asked carefully. "Before all this happened."

All this. It can't even be put into words, can it, James? She strove for a verbal reply. "I was afraid for her," she said honestly, knowing her feelings should not be held back because of sympathy. It seemed as though her father had changed. Certainly the devil-may-care look had entirely disappeared, leaving a devastating kind of wisdom in its place, but it was her mother's radiant and vulnerable features that kept entering her mind. Woman. The everlasting victim in love.

James exhaled a heavy breath. "You never were afraid to call a spade a spade," he said. "You take after your grandmother in that respect. She, of course, always knew I was no good."

"Don't do this, James," Elizabeth said abruptly.

"Do what?" He frowned at her.

"Play on my sympathies."

His eyes glinted a bit. "I have no need of your sympathy, Elizabeth," he told her. "It's your mother's forgiveness I'm hoping for."

Their eyes sparked at each other across the table. "You don't care how much you hurt her, do you? Just so long as you can wrap her around your little finger again!"

"You don't know what you're talking about, Elizabeth," James said, his voice steady. "I love your mother and you know that damned well."

"But it isn't the same for you as it is for her," she insisted.

"And what makes you say that? Because of the gambling?"

"In a way. Because I know that Mother would give up the world for you. But let me ask you a hypothetical question, James. Do you think it's wise for a woman to put all her eggs in one basket?"

"I don't know what you're getting at," James said, giving her a shake of his head.

"Of course you don't, because you've never had to do that—you've never had to stand helplessly by and watch the bottom fall out. Men never have to."

"Ah," James said, looking enlightened. "Women's liberation. Why didn't you say so?"

"Maybe because I knew you'd scoff at it, just as you're doing. Mother gave up her identity for you and that's all you can say? Well, you can rest assured, James, I'll never make those kinds of sacrifices for a man. Trust can have a mighty thin crust in most circumstances."

James looked at her for a long moment, and then slowly proceeded to slice through to the real core of the matter. "I don't think we're talking so much here about me and your mother," he said. "But if we were, I'd tell you that I've beaten myself to death on account of what I've done to her. I'd tell you that my heart aches so badly that I want to rip it out. I'd tell you that she's the only woman in this world for me, and that I've learned that life without her isn't any kind of life at all. I don't know if any of that helps you, and I don't know if I'm solely the one to blame for these fears you've developed.

But one thing I do know, Elizabeth, is that when that poet said the world was well lost for love, he damn well wasn't talking through his hat."

Elizabeth watched him, conscious of that lump forming in her throat again.

"And women aren't the only ones to fall victim to the beat of those jungle drums, Elizabeth," he finished.

5

It was twilight, and Elizabeth was sitting on the porch swing with the dog curled up at her feet. She had not seen Logan since the incident in his room, and she was conscious of feeling both impatience and expectancy.

"Some host," she muttered, nursing a glass of Clamato juice. "You'd think he'd at least have the decency to show up for the evening meals."

Tornado twitched his response.

Cooking odors still wafting on the evening breeze reminded Elizabeth that her services had not been welcomed or required in the kitchen. "And that cousin of his," she whispered to the dog. "You know what that's called, don't you? Reverse snobbery—that's what it's called. You know what she said to me? She said my high heels would make holes in the new cushion floor."

Tornado whined appropriately and thumped his tail twice.

"I know what you're thinking. You're wondering why I didn't bring my oxfords, or some Hush Puppies, at the very least. Oops, sorry about that, old fellow. Well, the answer is I wouldn't be caught dead in them and I forgot to bring slippers along. But I did offer to go barefoot, to no avail. Guess what, Tornado: 'It isn't proper.'"

The dog got stiffly to his feet and licked her hand.

"No, don't disturb yourself, old friend," she said fondly. "I know you're just collecting your pension these days. All you have to do is just lie there and listen. And you are an excellent listener, did you know that?" She scratched and ruffled his head and wondered about this sudden penchant for soliloquizing.

"Because, after all, if it weren't for you, I'd be talking to myself, wouldn't I? And that's always a sign, they say."

What was she doing here, anyway? Apart from the laughter she and James had shared, she had really only succeeded in making him feel worse about the whole situation. So much so that he had spent the remainder of the day off by himself, entertaining who knew what maudlin thoughts. He would have been better off if she'd stayed in Toronto.

Wonderful, Elizabeth. Why didn't you twist the knife a little more? Just because James tried to look recovered and capable didn't necessarily mean that he was. For all intents and purposes his world had just collapsed around his ears, and all she could do was spout off about what he'd done to her psyche. And force him to make promises that he might not be able to keep. What now? Would he pick up that gun again? It was so hard to imagine James doing such a thing, but he had.

And the loan! My God, she had completely forgotten about offering James the money to get back on his feet! Maybe he wouldn't have accepted it, but at least he would have known that she had faith in him, that she would give him all the support she could.

The sound of a vehicle coming up the drive reached her ears, and she twisted around expectantly, thinking that it would surely be Logan coming in from the range.

Or would he be on horseback? She didn't know. She only knew the person emerging from the small two-seater car definitely wasn't Logan. It was Kate Matthews.

Great, Elizabeth thought, remembering how the woman had been literally dripping with beer the last time she had seen her.

Kate walked briskly across the yard and then took the veranda steps with a bounce and energy that could only be accomplished in flat-heeled shoes.

Boots. Elizabeth corrected, when Kate stopped abruptly a few feet away from her.

"Oh," Kate said. "It's you."

Charming. Elizabeth smiled. "Yes. Yes, it is."

"Well. How are you?"

"At the moment? Bored."

"Then Logan isn't around?"

That was quick. "Afraid not."

"Where would he be this time of night?"

"I really don't know. I'm assuming he's out on the range rounding up the herd with the rest of his men. That is what they do this time of year, isn't it?"

"Yes," Kate said, her voice very clipped. "But Logan has good men to oversee the roundup. And it's rarely necessary for him to spend the night out there."

Elizabeth shrugged. "Then I'm afraid I'm blank." She was thinking that Kate's dark hair looked surprisingly good drawn back from her face in the inevitable ponytail. The style went well with the Gypsy brown eyes and the slightly wide mouth. There was a familiarity, too, in the shape of the nose and brow that had nothing to do with past acquaintance. Perhaps a model she knew. Kate wasn't classically pretty, but she could be very attractive with a little fixing up.

Kate's eyes met Elizabeth's directly. "Then do you suppose you could tell me Red's whereabouts? Or is that a blank, too?"

"Red?" Elizabeth questioned.

Kate's lips tightened before she spoke again. "Yes. Red. Logan's foreman. His right-hand man. Am I getting through to you Miss Jackson?"

"That's Ms." Elizabeth was playing for time. She had no wish to tell Kate that Logan had sent his foreman to oversee

Sweetwater in her father's absence. The horse farm was not that big an operation, but it did require some expert supervision, and Logan obviously felt Red was the best man for the job. She didn't want Kate to start questioning her on all this, feeling that James's gambling lapse was a private matter.

"I do beg your pardon," Kate replied, barely concealing her anger.

"That's quite all right," Elizabeth replied pleasantly, knowing she was taking all her pent-up feelings out on Kate. She supposed she ought to be feeling sorry for her—it was such a long drive back and forth between Logan's home and the general store Kate ran expressly for the ranch hands and their families. Yet apparently Kate was still doing it on a regular basis. She was obviously a very patient woman.

"I'm afraid I don't know where Red is, either," Elizabeth went on to say breezily, forgiving herself easily for the lie.

Kate looked as though she were mentally counting to ten, but not quite making it. "Listen," she said, controlling her voice with an effort. "I don't know why you still dislike me after all this time, and I don't really care. You have come a long way up in your world, so I hear, and that's fine. That's wonderful! Congratulations! So could you please tell me why you still consider me some sort of threat to you? There is no doubt in my mind that Red will still dance to your tune. The question I'm asking myself is why would you want him to? Or is it just that you require every man to fall at your feet?"

Elizabeth stared at Kate, then laughed a little. "Kate, what are we talking about here?"

"The mysterious disappearance of one or two men!" Kate exclaimed in a low voice. "And you know perfectly well where Red is—I can tell."

Elizabeth frowned a little. "Perhaps. But back up just a little. What did you mean about Red dancing to my tune? I don't understand what—"

"Oh, come off it, Elizabeth. You know perfectly well he was smitten with you. And the two of you were always going off somewhere together. So please drop the coy act. It doesn't suit you anymore."

Elizabeth's expression remained troubled and blank. "Red was always very friendly to me," she offered after a moment, wondering why they were even talking this way about the tall, rangy foreman.

"You're telling me you didn't know that Red was panting over you?" Kate questioned in apparent disbelief.

"Red wasn't in love with me," Elizabeth said with assurance.

"That isn't the word for it, no."

"Well, I didn't notice it, in any case."

"Now that I believe. I guess it is kind of hard to keep track, isn't it?"

Elizabeth put fingers to her brow. "Kate, forgive me for seeming dense, but I honestly don't know why we're having this particular discussion or argument, whatever it is. I can't tell you where Red is, but if you want to wait for Logan and question him on it, then be my guest. I can only assure you that I haven't got either of them locked in my bedroom."

Kate flinched a little at that, then went on to say, "But you are a houseguest here."

"For the moment, yes."

"Why aren't you staying at your father's place?"

"Because James is here, as well," Elizabeth said impatiently. "Is there anything else you'd like to know?"

"Yes," Kate answered immediately. "I would like to know what a woman like you sees in all this."

"All what? And what type am I being cast as?"

"I think I'd file you under *I* for *intruder*. You don't belong here, Elizabeth, regardless of how Logan feels about you."

"Sooner or later, I felt sure we'd get around to discussing Logan," Elizabeth responded, her features rigidly composed.

"Oh, yes. And I only wish there was some way I could effectively warn him about you."

"I just bet you do," Elizabeth replied, experiencing a sinking feeling because Kate's eyes were moist.

Kate shook her head as she turned on her heel. "With any luck at all, you'll be gone by the time I come around again."

"Kate," Elizabeth called, just as the other woman was about to take the stairs. "You're probably right about that. About my not staying here long."

Kate turned to her. "Good, Elizabeth. But why are you telling me this?"

"I guess because I agree with you. I know I really don't belong here. It's hard not to know when everybody keeps pointing it out so clearly."

Kate looked down at the steps for a moment, her profile in heavy shadow under the porchlights. "I'm sorry about that," she finally said, her flat tones making the words ambiguous. A moment later she was crossing the yard to her car.

"You're sorry," Elizabeth breathed.

The collie placed his paw on her knee and whined.

She looked down at the dog, her vision becoming blurred. "Thanks," she whispered. "I really needed that."

Elizabeth had a nightcap with a very subdued James, whose silence screamed out to her that he'd rather be alone with his thoughts. She climbed the stairs heavily, then decided to make a fast search of his room in case there were any stray guns lying around. After reassuring herself, she went into her room and, still fully clothed in the jeans and blouse she had put on earlier in the day, lay down on the bed.

She wondered if James had been preparing to phone her mother tonight. That would explain his preoccupation. He would be trying to summon up the courage, in addition to carefully rehearsing what would have to be said. Elizabeth could imagine him walking the floor, right at this moment, gradually coming closer to the phone, until his hand would eventually rest on the receiver.

No, James! Not yet. Don't burst the bubble yet.

She wished Logan would come home and talk to him. She wished Logan would come home and talk to her! *He offers to help, and then what does he do? Takes off for the entire day!*

She got to her feet and began to pace, feeling restless and weighted with depression. Was it absolutely imperative that her mother be told? Did she have to be hurt?

"Any life he offered me was better than the stultifying existence here!"

Those were her mother's exact words to Rose Claybourne...but had she really meant them? *"There isn't going to be any slipup,"* she had told Elizabeth with such complete assurance that there had been no room for argument.

Aloud, Elizabeth said softly, "In other words, even if there was, you wouldn't want to hear about it, would you, Mother? You would choose not to know."

Because Catherine would marry James, anyway. Elizabeth suddenly knew this with certainty. Her mother would remarry her father no matter what because that was, and always had been, the only clear path her feet could take. She would take it lightly and joyfully or she would take it because there wasn't any other choice for her, except the half-living state she had referred to as a stultifying existence. But she would take it.

Elizabeth opened her bedroom door and ran down the hallway to the stairs. Logan was at the foot of them, dust streaked and sun weathered, his foot on the first step. He glanced up at her.

"Logan!" she said, quickly running down and missing the sudden light that entered his eyes. "I'm so glad you're home I—"

Before she could say anything else, his arms came out and around her, sweeping her up and turning her until she was settled against his rough length.

"Now that's what I call a greeting," he murmured, looking down into her wide eyes. "It was worth staying away so long."

She frowned at him. "I meant to speak to you about that also. You told me the two of us were going to put our heads together and talk—"

A warm, vibrant kiss halted her flow of words momentarily.

"About James," she finished, her eyes falling to the sensual curve of his lips in a belated reaction, her body still feeling the disturbing effects of them.

"I know, I didn't mean to stay out this late," he apologized. "Not when it's taken me so long to find the ways and means to get you out here. But there was some trouble out on—"

"Hold it," Elizabeth said. "What you just said about 'ways and means'—how does that fit in with James's trouble?"

"It fits in, that's all. Why? Are you thinking that it's all a hoax?" Logan shook his head. "That isn't what I meant to imply. Just think of yourself as the silver lining in this particular cloud. I'm not happy about James's problems, but I am glad that they've brought you here."

Elizabeth looked at him wordlessly, knowing she was in danger of becoming lost in the tawny depths of his eyes.

"Stay the summer with me, Elizabeth. Can you?"

"I..."

"A month, then. Can you free yourself for a month?"

"Logan...you aren't giving me a chance to think. I need to talk to James right now. He's about to phone Mother and I don't think he should. You don't know my mother. She...she irrevocably tied to James. He's just got to lick this thing so he can't hurt her anymore, but I don't think he should tell her about this because—"

Once again, Logan halted her words with a kiss, one that lingered for quite some time.

"James isn't phoning anyone, Liz'beth. He's sitting out on the porch," His mouth was grazing hers now, where before it had devoured. His hands were gently persuasive as he stroked her slender back. "I spoke to him for a bit. He told me he was going to go for a walk and then turn in." His eyes moved over her, taking in the Gypsy hoops in her ears, the warm, creamy flesh at her throat where the pink silk blouse parted. "So you see?" he murmured. "You can hold off on that particular worry until morning." The intensity in his eyes increased. "So could we talk about us now?"

"Us?" Elizabeth's blue gaze glanced off him, as if searching for some other distraction.

"For starters," he said huskily, "Do you have any idea how delicious you look in pink? How does it manage to go so well with your dark red hair?"

"Logan, do you realize you have me absolutely covered in grime and dust?" she replied instead.

He looked down at where their bodies met. "High-fashion model and cow man," he mused. "We don't go so well together, do we, Liz? Have I ruined your blouse entirely?"

She shook her head far too quickly. "I don't mind, Logan, really."

"I should have cleaned up before I even touched you. One faux pas after another, I'm afraid." His mouth formed a dry line. "Prince Charming I'm not."

Elizabeth, feeling angry at herself for her stupid comment, said, "You always manage to surprise me. I mean, faux pas, for goodness' sake? Not to mention fait accompli? And here I am worrying about a little dust and grime? What do you do, Logan, practice this extensive vocabulary on your cattle? Even in my grandmother's drawing room, you would fit right in. Clothes, and the dust on them, do not make the man."

He didn't immediately respond, but she knew her words had registered all the same. "Liz'beth, you shouldn't say those things to me. It might give me unmanageable ideas."

She smiled up at him. "Maybe you ought to become a writer."

Something flickered in his eyes, but then it was gone, his smile dry again as he said, "Cattleman-turned-author. Now that would really be one for the books, wouldn't it?"

"Guaranteed to get you into *Who's Who*," she returned.

His features took on that stony look of old, blanking her out as he said, "Let's get off this ridiculous subject, all right?"

His abrupt change of mood seemed tantamount to a slap in the face, and Elizabeth drew back in his arms accordingly, her eyes not entirely disguising the effects of his tone on her.

He frowned and swore a little under his breath, before bringing her against him once again. "I didn't want to spoil this," he said, his voice softening as he touched his lips to her brow. "Don't let my roughness put you off, all right, sweetheart? I want to take you upstairs. If you'll wait while I get cleaned up, then we can talk, all right?"

Once again she felt warm and cared for, highly conscious of the endearment he had used and how easily he could settle her ruffled feelings. She shouldn't let him get to her like this. She knew that. And yet temptation was so high, so achingly high.

"Talk?" she questioned throatily, knowing she had to make some sort of stand, weak though it was.

"Get better acquainted," he qualified, his voice husky. "Maybe we have a lot more in common than either of us thinks," he said suggestively.

She had to fight with herself, but finally she managed to shake her head. Her recent encounter with Kate helped her with the decision. Thoughts of Charles came up a slow second.

"I don't think we should get any better acquainted, Logan." She managed to voice the words without too much hesitation. "I realize what you're asking, and...well, I don't go in for casual sex. Then there's Charles, of course."

"You're really serious about him?" he questioned, his jaw looking ominously rigid.

She nodded firmly.

"Why don't I believe you?"

"I can't imagine."

"Stay here for the summer, Liz'beth," he said again. "If you're that serious about Durney, he'll have you for the rest of your life. I'm only asking for a crumb in comparison."

"You're asking me to sleep with you."

"Is that the moon?"

"It's a highly important facet of a relationship to me. I told you, I don't go in for casual sex."

He looked down at her steadily, his eyes dark. "It could never be casual, Elizabeth. Not between you and me."

Which was exactly what she was afraid of. And an entire summer of it? How could she bear that?

"You'll have to let me think about it awhile."

He lowered his mouth to hers in a slow kiss of deep persuasion, his hands and his body still, only his mouth filling her with sensual lethargy. "Then tonight is out of the question?" he murmured, when her head remained thrown back, her eyes closed.

"Yes," she breathed, giving the right answer to the wrong question. It surprised her, therefore, when he said in soft resignation, "You can't blame a man for trying. Will you do one little thing for me, though?"

She opened her eyes to look blankly at him.

"Wash my back in the shower?" he said, his eyes not entirely teasing.

It got through to her then—what she had been agreeing to in her mind. A cold shower for her would better fill the bill.

She stepped out of his arms, knowing it was her only safe bet, and managing an adequate degree of coolness, she replied, "I certainly won't do that. But if you behave yourself, I'll willingly escort you to the shower and bring up a nice cold beer to add to your refreshment. How's that?"

"Sounds promising," he murmured. "But you won't scrub my back?"

She shook her head. "When and if..."

"You realize what you're doing to me, don't you?"

If her own feelings were any judge, she thought she knew pretty well. "Feminine power is fun. Haven't you heard, Logan?"

"Then, too," he said, "there are some men who won't let you put that particular hoop through their nose."

"Want to bet?" she said.

"No," he returned, looking appropriately subdued.

"WHERE'S YOURS?" he said, when she handed him a cold mug of beer through a small slit in the shower curtain.

"I'm abstaining for the rest of the week."

"How come?"

"I got plastered on the plane during my flight."

"You're kidding."

"Unfortunately, no. Heights are an extreme weakness of mine."

"I didn't know that."

"Now you do. I'll grab any kind of help that's available—and I suffer for it afterward."

"That's why you always used to take a train out to see James," he mused.

"That's why. So tell me, Logan, since you wanted us to become better acquainted, what are your vulnerable points?"

"You."

"I'm serious."

"So am I. You play hell with me, Liz'beth. You always have."

The shadow of his body through the shower curtain was too tempting taken in conjunction with his words, so she turned away. "And what about Kate? Aren't you vulnerable where she is concerned, too?"

She heard him swear softly through the muffling rain of the shower.

"For the last time, Elizabeth," he finally said. "Kate has no bearing on you and me."

"I think she might disagree with you."

The shower curtain slid open violently. "Forget Kate!"

She swung around and stared at him, wishing he did not look nearly as good as he did. Dripping, stark-naked wet, he was an Adonis calling up an answering cry deep in her subconsciousness.

"I can't. She was here today. Again. As usual!"

"Because she has the perfect right."

"Why?" she asked, keeping her vision trained above his belt line.

"Because my father sowed a few seeds where he shouldn't have, that's why. Satisfied? She wouldn't thank me for telling you. Not you of all people."

Elizabeth's jaw had dropped. "You mean that Kate is...your sister?" she finished on a rising note.

Logan grabbed a towel and tied it around his middle as he stepped over the tub. "My half sister," he qualified. "Illegitimate," he added. "It's no deep, dark secret, but nobody talks about it because they know how sensitive Kate is. After my parents passed on, I tried my best to make her a part of all this, but she wouldn't have any of it. She hated my father for what he had done to her mother. I wasn't too proud of him myself. That's why your remark about my father putting my mother up on a pedestal filled me with a grim sort of humor.

She was a half-breed to him and always would be. And you can't really cheat on a half-breed, can you?" His words were heavy with irony.

Elizabeth backed up as he advanced on her. "So," he went on softly, "now all the skeletons are out of the closet. Do you still think I'd fit into your grandmother's drawing room?"

Backing her up against the vanity, he placed his hands on either side of her head, threading his fingers through her hair as he read every nuance of her expression.

"You should have told me," she managed bravely. "I...I've been impossibly rude to Kate for the most ridiculous of all reasons."

"For decency's sake I won't even ask what reasons, but I think you ought to know that Kate is in love with Red and always has been."

"Red," Elizabeth repeated, as though it were a memory lesson.

"Red. Who once had the hots for you, I might add. Why do you think I got rid of him by sending him out to your father's place? My right-hand man, Elizabeth. That's the reason I had to stay away so long tonight. There are other men who would have filled the bill as far as Sweetwater was concerned."

Feeling impossibly stupid, Elizabeth could only stare at him. She felt as though she had just stepped into a high drama that had been taking place all around her, with herself being entirely unaware. She knew it would do her no good—as had been the case with Kate—to tell him that she'd had no idea of Red's feelings toward her. She'd had no idea because, at the age of nineteen, she had been totally swept up in the lure of Logan.

And it was no wonder, she told herself now, feeling surrounded by his masculinity—feeling overwhelmed by his raw sensuality. His hold on her head held her prisoner for whatever he decided to do next—and she found herself hoping that it had something to do with his near-naked form and the intensity of his expression.

"And do you know what else I wish I could do?" he said. "I wish I could send the elite Charles Durney, hail fellow well met, to the far corners of the earth. And maybe he ought to distribute his money around while he's there. I thought I was a rich man until I got hold of that *Who's Who* registry. You've got Fort Knox sleeping in your bed, don't you, Elizabeth?"

She felt it was safer not to respond in any way.

"There's just one last thing you ought to know about me—just to really round out our *acquaintanceship*, you understand: I lied to you about the gun business, Elizabeth. James doesn't own a gun, so naturally it would be impossible for him to pick it up and try to kill himself with it. That's all I lied about, but I knew it would be enough. I knew it would bring you flying out here."

She stared at him for a slow and steady count of five seconds—and then her face contorted furiously. "You did what?"

"I think you heard me pretty well."

She twisted her head away and out of his grasp. "I could hope to be mistaken, though!"

"I stand guilty."

She had to get out of there. Logan was looking many things, but guilty was not one of them.

"All's fair in love and war," he told her softly.

And no doubt, he expected her to buy that for a literal truth. "There's a big difference between love and lust, Logan," she told him angrily. "But neither one would excuse you from that particular agony of worry you put me through! I knew James would never do a thing like that. But then, you were so convincing weren't you? And telling me not to mention it to James because he couldn't even remember doing it! Someone should hang you!"

"I guess I knew you'd take it this way," he said as she marched to the door that led to her bedroom.

"Congratulations on your astuteness!" she said, slamming the door in his face.

AT BREAKFAST THE FOLLOWING MORNING, she tried hard to ignore Logan's presence, though she was thankful that it caused Elvira to hum cheerfully as she set down the platters of food.

"Why doesn't she eat with us?" she said to a spot just past Logan's left ear.

"Why don't you ask her?" Logan suggested.

"Why don't I just dump this platter of eggs over my head instead?"

"That bad, huh?"

"Elizabeth has the notion that Elvira doesn't like her," James put in.

"Elizabeth is correct," Elizabeth said.

"I'll speak to her," Logan said.

"Don't you dare!" she returned swiftly. "Just tell her to please sit down at a table she's worked so hard over."

"Elizabeth," Logan said slowly. "You should understand that, cousin or no, Elvira works for me. She enjoys her job and feels very proud of the table she sets. But she wouldn't sit down at it any more than your grandmother's employees would sit down at hers. Elvira's two sons are employed on this ranch. So was her layabout husband, until he took off on her. Then there's Conch, Wooden Leg and Chief George—all distant relatives of mine. If I had them all sit down at the table with their families, there wouldn't be room for me or my guests."

"That's kind of the way I had it figured," James said.

Elizabeth turned her glare on him. "Oh, you did, did you?"

James put his piece of bacon down. "Elizabeth, what's with you?" he said.

Elizabeth looked at her untouched plate. "Oh, lots and lots of things, James."

"James," Logan said. "I think it only fair to tell you that I told Elizabeth, in a manner of speaking, that you had put a gun to your head."

"What?" James turned to Logan slowly.

Logan nodded. "Sorry. It seemed the only sure way to get her out here."

After a moment or two, James responded. "In that case, then, I guess you can be forgiven."

"Oh, he can, can he?" Elizabeth glared at James.

"Now, Elizabeth..." James began.

She threw down her napkin and rose to her feet. "Don't you try and placate me! I was worried sick about you! I even checked your room last night for guns! I knew I wouldn't sleep a wink if I didn't!" She turned to Logan, her temper giving her dark red hair its credibility. "You may think all this is a fine coup on your part—but I beg to differ!"

"Elizabeth," Logan said, rising, also. "I don't. Believe me."

"Believe you? I might as well believe James's sob story!"

James, looking a little lost, rose, too. "Can't we discuss this calmly?" he said.

Elizabeth rounded on her father. "Why? So you can bring another tear to my eye? And why are you here, come to think of it? Why here at Logan's? You don't need any death-watch services, do you? You came because Logan invited you into his intrigue, didn't you? After all, you're an old hand at this. I should have known it was all a big con job! You wash Logan's back and he'll wash yours! He'll get you out of debt, and in the meantime you'll have the opportunity to not only sell your daughter down the river, but enlist her sympathies, as well!"

"You've got it all wrong, Elizabeth," Logan said heavily, while James looked on white faced. "I may have conned you a little, but James certainly hasn't."

"You must think I'm a first-class fool!" She looked at one then the other, her temper blinding her to the truth in James's face. "But then I already knew that two of you were far too much alike!" She turned and made a swift and furious passage out of the room.

James looked over at Logan.

"I know, I know," he said, sinking down.

James subsided more slowly. "I guess I should have warned you about that temper of hers. In a lot of ways, she takes after her grandmother. Her mother, too, come to think of it."

"Now you tell me."

"That's all I've told you. And you'd damn well better make Elizabeth realize it. If you hadn't got me so drunk the other night, I wouldn't have agreed to any part of this."

"THE REASON I'M AT LOGAN'S," James told Elizabeth succinctly, when she was prepared to listen, "is because I had the hangover of a lifetime when I woke up here the following morning. He told me that he'd get Dadblastit back for me if I did him one small, tiny favor. Naturally I asked him what."

"Naturally," Elizabeth mouthed, allowing James to walk alongside her. She had gone outside to cool her head, walking along the stretch of forest land that skirted the back of Logan's property.

"He said that all the interest he required was that I spend a week or two at his place. He said he needed my presence to ensure yours."

"You aren't making me feel the least bit better, James."

"Aren't I? Don't you feel a little flattered by Logan's wish to have you visit out here?"

"No, I don't! I feel like a fool."

"And you're thinking that I conned you, too, aren't you?"

She remembered her father's devastated look at the breakfast table and shook her head. "I think I was probably wrong about that."

"Honey, Logan could have led me off the side of a cliff that night and I wouldn't have known the difference. I wouldn't have asked why, either, because, in a manner of speaking, the man staked his reputation on me. I figured anything he asked was the least I could do. Besides, you used to enjoy coming out here."

"I guess I understand," she said grudgingly.

"But you still don't entirely trust me, do you?"

"Oh, James," she said, feeling more than a little wiped out, "I knew the moment I said what I did that I'd done you an injustice. I guess I'm just beating around the bush about saying I'm sorry."

"Apology accepted," James said, squeezing her hand.

They walked in silence for a while, and then Elizabeth said, "I really don't think you should tell Mother, you know."

"You don't?"

"No. I think you should marry her and then spend the rest of your life trying to make her as happy as possible."

"That's what I intended to do."

"You still could, with the help of Gamblers Anonymous."

"You think it's that simple?"

"No. I think it's that necessary. Mother is going to fade away altogether if you don't smarten up, James."

"I hear what you're saying, Elizabeth."

"I hope so. You do realize that Mother doesn't care a thing about material wealth, don't you? Say it, James. Make me know you believe it."

"I guess it isn't a question of her caring," he returned slowly. "It's me. I never could bear the thought of Catherine doing without. I wanted to be able to give her everything that—"

"You took away from her on the day you married her?" Elizabeth finished immediately. "Oh, Dad, do you realize how boringly old-fashioned and traditional that makes you?"

James looked at her with raised eyebrows. "Oh, it does, eh?"

"Yes," she insisted.

"Getting tough with the old man, aren't you?"

"If it will do any good."

"Keep going."

"I guess you're so old-fashioned because you've been stuck out here in the boonies for so long. The world has changed that much," she said, opening her hands wide. Then she shook her head. "I never thought I'd see the day when James Jackson would become an anachronism."

"A what? Watch that mouth of yours."

"You know very well what it means. It means a thing or person out of its place or time. It means the old, let's-put-her-up-on-a-pedestal type of thinking. Or the old no-wife-of-mine-is-gonna-scrub-floors-on-her-hands-and-knees macho stuff. Well, what you do nowadays, James, is get down on your knees and scrub the floor with her. Blow soapsuds on each other and then have a crack-the-wet-rag contest. It's fun, and sooner or later the floor will get cleaned."

"You don't say? A crack-the-rag contest, eh?"

"Let your imagination be your guide," she tossed in, slanting a look in his direction.

James cleared his throat. "You're getting a little ahead of me now. I've been living out in the boonies, remember? And who have you been picking all this up from, may I ask?"

"If you're asking me who my man of the moment is, it really doesn't have any bearing on all this. Charles Durney is filthy rich."

"Durney, eh? Yes, I think your mother mentioned him in one of her letters. His father's some kind of financial wizard or something."

"Charles is no slouch, either."

James made a sound under his breath. "For a while there you had me buying all this, Elizabeth. Good try. And maybe I'll still give it some serious thought. But let's face it, honey, a good bank account never hurt any man's chances, and your Durney sounds like pretty good proof of that. I bet your grandmother is pleased, too."

Elizabeth stopped and frowned at him. "My liking for Charles has nothing to do with his bank account; it never did. I earn my own way in this life and I enjoy doing it, so whether a man has a lot of money is nothing to me. And why, James, does everything have to come back to Grandmother? I swear, you and Logan have a fixation on her."

"I think you've exhausted yourself today, Madame Freud, with that statement. If I seem fixated on her, it's probably because I feel a grudging respect for the old bat. She saw clear through me all those years ago and warned Catherine accordingly. The fact that she was right is what's so hard to accept."

"Then prove her wrong, James, once and for all. I know you can do it."

"And you don't think that your mother deserves to know about the faith I broke?" He was frowning.

"'Deserves,' can be a double-edged sword. Does she 'deserve' to be hurt again?"

"It would be cowardly not to tell her," James insisted.

"And yet, telling her could be construed by some as a way to ease a guilty conscience. Confession is good for the soul, but rarely does it make the other person feel better. As you said, by gambling again you broke the faith. Maybe you need to live with that unpalatable thought all by yourself. Live with it long and hard. Does that sound cowardly?"

"Elizabeth, you're getting too smart for me," James said slowly.

"If I thought telling Mother would do the least bit of good, I wouldn't advise you against it, James. On the other hand, I can tell you this much with full certainty. If you ever break your promise to her again, you can stop referring to me as your daughter. I simply will not allow you to break my mother's heart again. Not if there is any possible way I can prevent it."

"WHERE DO YOU THINK YOU'RE GOING?" Logan said, opening the door on her packing activities.

"Please knock before entering my room," she said coldly.

He moved back a step and knocked loudly on the opened door. "Now, where do you think you're going?" he asked again, moving into the room.

"The charade is over, remember? And James is going to get all the support he needs from the G.A. meeting he's attending tonight. Tomorrow he intends to return to Sweetwater to tally his assets—a mare and a yearling, to be exact—that he's pretty sure he has a buyer for. He intends to give you half the selling price as a down payment on Dadblastit, and I intend to be back in Toronto by first light."

"And how do you propose to get to the airport?" Logan demanded.

"James will take me when he goes to his meeting."

"So you've arranged everything?"

"Just as fast and as well as I was able."

He reached out and slammed shut her suitcase. "You aren't going, Elizabeth," he said flatly.

She looked down at the closed case and then up at him, her lips parting a little in amazement. "Are you going to tie me up and gag me, then?"

For the first time in all the years she had known him, a helpless look crossed his face. He dragged his hand through his hair as he said, "Of course not. You'll just have to accept and know that I'm not thinking too straight these days. Was the lie I told you unforgivable? I don't even know that much."

"Logan," she said softly, feeling an unaccountable urge to run to him, to throw her arms around him. "There are all sorts of reasons why I have to go."

His eyes were dark steadily burning flames as he looked at her. "I had to watch you walk away from me once before, Liz'beth. I don't think I can do it again."

"Don't say these things to me," she begged him, trying desperately to keep herself rooted in place. "I can't let myself get involved with you."

"Then feel pity for me, Liz'beth, because I've never stopped feeling involved with you."

She took one step toward him and then another, but when he looked as though he were going to reach out for her, she stopped and shook her head. "I can't let this happen," she breathed. "You've become too smooth, Logan. You know all the right things to say to a woman, don't you?"

"Do I? I don't seem to be having much luck with you. My sincerity had absolutely no effect."

She looked at him, trying to gauge his expression. "I...I don't know you anymore," she confessed. "You confuse me. Things are going on in your head that I can't even guess at."

"Elizabeth," he said huskily, "you have only to touch me and I become an open book."

She lowered her lashes for a moment, not able to make contact with his eyes. "Oh, sex," she said, in a deliberately offhand manner. "Is that what we're talking about here?"

"Among other things. The air is usually thick with it. Or haven't you noticed?"

She had, of course. Some things never changed, least of all the electricity that sizzled and crackled between them. And Elizabeth noticed it was becoming harder to ignore. She had been viewing him furtively, secretly, in much the same way as a child does a forbidden stick of candy. In indigo-denim shirt and jeans, Logan seemed at odds with the feminine trappings of her room. Dangerously and disturbingly at odds.

"No, I hadn't noticed," she said, still not meeting his eyes directly.

"Liar," he murmured, and then he was closing the gap, reaching for her.

"Logan. Don't," she gasped, as his arms encircled her. "Don't make it any harder."

"That's the first encouraging thing I've heard from you." He allowed her a little freedom within the imprisoning band of his arms. "Just stay the summer, Elizabeth. I won't ask any more of you than that."

She knew she had to make the protest while she still had the strength. "You don't have time for guests, remember?"

"What I said," he replied, "is that I haven't had time for the beach. But for you, I'll make the time."

His nearness was too intoxicating. His mouth, so near hers, so promising.... Desperately seeking a diversion, she said, "Oh? And where is there a beach around here?"

"Quit trying to sidetrack me," he murmured, moving in on her lips with firm possession. He seared her softly parting lips with a hot, moist kiss that was both persuasive and heart stopping, igniting her emotions, creating a slow-building fire in her loins. Then his tongue was slipping through her defenses, stoking the fire and fanning a breathless passion between them.

Her arms moved around his shoulders while he brought her tightly against him, his hands molding her waist and then moving down to the curve of her hips.

She could feel his hardness against her, and it was igniting every sensitized inch of her body. She moved against him subtly, experimentally, and she immediately heard his soft groan and felt the lowering of his hands to her buttocks. She drew back from the fiery torture of his mouth, a protest on her lips as he fitted her against him, but he wouldn't let her utter it.

His voice liquid with desire, he challenged, "Tell me again that you don't feel it in the air—that you don't know what has to happen between us."

"I don't have to tell you anything," she said, making an attempt to remove his hands. It was like trying to pry loose steel clamps.

"Dynamite jeans," he muttered huskily.

"Logan. Let go of me. Just because I...I don't mind kissing you, doesn't mean—"

He laughed softly. "You don't mind? Are you sure about that Liz? I'd hate to think I was forcing you to kiss me back like that."

"Let go of me," she demanded hotly, straining against his hands.

"I will if you promise to stay." He was watching the rise and fall of her breasts, the material of her striped shirt pulled taut across them.

"And have to fight you off like this every day? What would be the sense of that?"

"You don't have to fight, Liz'beth." His hands moved on her, and for an instant he was feeling the damp heat between her legs, feeling her longing through the fabric of her jeans.

She gasped and jerked back, staring at him, her cheeks burning. Then she slapped his face.

Instead of releasing her, however, he brought his hands up to her shoulders, catching her before she could step away. His eyes were steady, flickering flames as he met her angry, embarrassed gaze.

"I can't hide what you do to me," he told her. "You have only to look at me. Why is it so terrible for you to feel the same way?"

"I don't feel the same way! And I want you to leave my room right now! How dare you think you can touch me anytime you feel like it?"

He sighed heavily as he released her. "Maybe because I dream about you touching me. Believe me, Elizabeth, I would never slap you away."

"Oh, this is impossible!" She brought her hands to her face. "You are impossible, Logan. Six years ago you wouldn't even let me kiss you."

"I'm not a Boy Scout anymore. And you're not a naive girl."

"A Boy Scout," she said on a bitter laugh. "No, I certainly can't accuse you of that." She looked at him a little helplessly, secretly loving him with her eyes.

"Do whatever you want to me, Liz'beth," he said, meeting the look that she couldn't quite hide. "Tease me, torture me—get your revenge on what happened in the past. I promise not to lay a hand on you unless you ask me to."

How could a mere man look so tempting, she wondered. And how had he managed to zero in on a very strong fantasy of hers—one that she had unconsciously entertained more times than she cared to admit? Her very own living, breathing, Logan doll.

She smiled a little ruefully. In her fantasy, the first thing she generally required of him—after she had placed her lips softly against the corner of his mouth—was that he strip.

"Sorry," she murmured. "You don't deserve such punishment."

"Curse the luck," he muttered.

Nonetheless, she went over to him and kissed the cheek that she had slapped. When she looked up at him she almost melted under his gaze.

Before she knew it, she was kissing the same spot again, and then his chin felt the butterfly softness. She rested her palms lightly on his shoulders as her lips touched the corner of his mouth engaged in a secret sojourn of her own.

"Sweet," she heard him murmur. "And you smell like lemons."

"Put your arms around me, Logan."

He obliged immediately and she felt his firm warmth. Her lips curved gently. "Now back me over to the bed."

"I hope I don't knock you over in my haste."

"If you do, you'll just have to waste time and energy picking me up."

The back of her thighs hit the mattress as he said, "Here we are, safe and sound."

"Don't crush me in the fall, that's all I ask."

He followed those instructions to the letter, bracing himself above her on the softness of the bed. He used one hand to push her suitcase well out of the way, and then she was feeling the entire length of him as he settled himself carefully against her, his forearms resting on the bed on either side of her head, creating a dizzying intimacy as he looked down at her.

His breath moved the wisps of hair from her brow and cheek. "Comfortable?" he whispered, his knee insinuating itself between hers.

She moved her head up and down.

"What do you want me to do next?"

"Nothing. I've tortured you enough."

He looked down at her for a long moment. "You don't want to give me precise instructions on how you'd like to be kissed?"

She bit her lip to prevent a smile and shook her head.

His eyes followed the nibbling action. "What would happen if I took matters into my own hands?"

"Then I'd know you were entirely untrustworthy, and I wouldn't stay." The moment the last part of her statement was out, she knew she had just committed herself unintentionally.

"Then you will stay." He pounced before she could take back her words.

She looked at him beseechingly.

He shook his head. "No way. I'm not letting you out of this."

"Logan, you're forgetting about...you know—Charles."

His expression took on a slightly grim cast. "I wish to hell I could. But you keep bringing him up, Liz'beth."

"I can't help it. I feel distinctly guilty about this. And about...what might happen if I stay here. You've been stalking me ever since I arrived, and I'm beginning to feel like a cornered mouse. What are my chances of escape, Logan?"

"Very slim, I'd say."

"But you can understand why I'd have to talk the matter over with Charles." At the moment it seemed a very slim wedge, but she decided to use her relationship with Charles for all it was worth.

All mellowness had left his expression. He raised himself up, the better to stare down at her. "What are you telling me? That you and he have made firm commitments to each other?"

"I did make him certain promises, yes," she replied, feeling a definite waning of his warmth. She wanted to reach out and bring him back to her. Closely back.

"About what? Marriage?"

She shook her head. "No...not yet."

Logan frowned. "Then what? Living together?"

Elizabeth stared at him realizing that she couldn't tell him that she and Charles had not even slept together yet. Logan already seemed to be holding so many advantages where her emotions and her body were concerned. All she had was her mind and her secrets and the clarity of future projections. If she were to spend any time at all with him, she had to keep the inevitable ending in clear view: her eventual return to Charles and to a profession that had been good to her. A deep involvement with Logan would threaten the very fabric of her existance.

6

"YES," Elizabeth replied. "Plans to live together. That is, we've discussed them."

Logan got off the bed and stood broodingly looking down at her. "How can you respond to me the way you do if you're all tied up with another man?" He shook his head. "Something doesn't add up here."

She sat up slowly, chastising herself for creating the web of lies this was becoming. "In the first place, I don't consider my response to you in any way special, and in the second—"

"Elizabeth," he broke in, "whether you want to admit it or not, the fact of the matter is you turn into molten lava if I so much as touch you. So could we have some honesty here? Either you're a hot little number with every man you meet, or you've got one hell of a half-baked relationship going with Prince Charming."

"Don't call him that!" she said, her cheeks flaming. "And I'll thank you to keep your opinions to yourself! As it happens, neither one of us—Charles or myself—feels that sex is the be-all and end-all of a relationship! In fact—" she leaped from the bed and gave him a shove "—I've often thought I could get by in this life very well without it! So don't you dare call me a 'hot little number'!" she finished furiously.

Logan's lips twitched slightly, halting Elizabeth, who had been preparing to push him physically out of her room.

"What's so funny?" She was still angry, but momentarily taken aback.

He seized her waist, lifting her in the air until she stood on the bed holding his shoulders to keep her balance.

"Logan! What on earth are you doing?"

"Putting you on a pedestal."

She shook her head at him in a gesture of hopelessness. "I don't understand you."

"No. But I understand you. Better than Durney ever will."

She frowned at him. "I really don't want to discuss him with you anymore."

"I'm not too concerned about him anymore, either," he said, his eyes mellow and teasing.

"I don't know what you're looking so damned pleased about." She was trying to recall precisely what she had said, but nothing was coming through other than a jumble of angry words she'd uttered in response to his "hot little number" accusation. She could have sworn, however, that she had defended herself well.

Logan, having composed his features, replied blandly, "Nothing much, it was just the way you looked when you were trying to beat me up. Do you realize that in the space of twenty minutes or so, you've slapped me, tortured me and tried to bulldoze me?"

She couldn't stop the smile that curved her lips. "You deserved it all, and more. Logan, for heaven's sake, get me down from here. Must you he-man types forever and always prove your physical strength?"

"There you go, little lady," he said in a broad drawl as he set her back down on the floor.

"One thing I can say about you," she muttered a little breathlessly. "You are not a dull man. In that respect, you are just like my father."

"Is that what you meant when you accused of us of being too much alike?"

"Oh—" She laughed lightly. "Perhaps. I rarely know *what* I say when I lose my temper."

He made no response, other than to say quietly, "I hope I don't have James to overcome, as well."

She flashed him a scathing look. "I'm going to pretend you didn't say that."

"I only meant that you tend to put a man through hoops before you'll really trust him."

It was an insightful comment and one that she couldn't deny. "I suppose James *can* be blamed for that," she snapped, turning toward to her half-filled suitcase. She opened it and looked at the contents. "It would be better if I went to stay at Sweetwater, you know. We...we could probably see each other from time to time. I would stay until the wedding, if that's still going to take place, but..."

Logan was shaking his head. "I want you as my house-guest. And if you want it to be hands off, then I'll try to oblige you. But the other part has already been settled. Red will be back here to take over if James is so set on returning home. In fact, I'll make the call right now. That means I'll have the time to indulge your every whim, Liz'beth. Whatever you want to do, wherever you want to go, I'm available and will-ing to please. I heard you telling James you hadn't had a va-cation in two years, so take the one I'm offering you. It's free. And there won't be any strings."

To have Logan all to herself whenever she wanted him was a pretty heady thought. It was also a dangerous one.

"I don't put much credence in those last few words."

"That doesn't mean I won't want to make love to you," he qualified. "But it will be up to you if we do or not. A no from you will stop me dead in my tracks, Liz'beth."

"Do you mean that?"

"I do. And take this into consideration, too. I could use a vacation myself—a rest from the ranch."

"All right." The words were out before she could have sec-ond thoughts. "If you mean all that you say, I'll take you up on your company and your hospitality." Her eyes lingered on his mouth, then moved to the safer regions of his throat. "No doubt we'll spend most of our time arguing, though, about one thing or another."

"Never a dull moment, as they say," he returned quietly, his eyes, too, dwelling for several moments on her lips.

She acknowledged his statement with only a blink of her eyes.

It was he who moved away first. "So...we have a whole afternoon ahead of us, Elizabeth. What would you like to do?"

"I don't know. What do you suggest?"

"How about a ride into the mountains?"

She looked at him, her eyes lighting up. "Do you realize how long it's been since I've ridden a horse?"

"Then I'll have to pick a real gentle nag for you, I guess."

She frowned playfully. "What will that do to my image?"

"Steady Joe, then," he said, smiling at her. "A true gentleman, and a gelding to help the cause."

She raised her eyebrows. "Maybe you ought to take a few lessons from him, Logan."

He smiled. "I haven't had the benefits of castration, my lovely greenhorn."

Her face colored as she sputtered, "Of course I knew that—" Breaking off with an impatient sound, she concluded; "There are some things best left unsaid."

"But then I'd never get to see that amazing blush of yours, would I?" he teased.

"Madman. I never blush."

"So you'd like me to believe."

"Could we take along a picnic lunch? I'm starving." It was as good a change of subject as any.

"Whatever your heart desires. I'll tell Elvira to fix us something. I don't suppose you could get a bathing suit on under those tight jeans of yours?"

Her hands smoothed the hips of the ocher denims she had struggled into that morning. "Why?"

He raised his eyes to her face. "There aren't any beaches around here, as you know." He grinned. "But there is a dandy swimming hole I could take you to. Maybe that way I'll even get used to the sight of you scantily clad."

"You may. I just so happen to have an extremely tiny bikini along with me."

"I'm to be tortured again, then," he murmured, his eyes moving over the length of her high-breasted, long-legged figure. "In fact, a man could die from this. I thought all models were supposed to be flat-chested and skinny?"

"You're dreadfully out of date, Logan." She tossed her hair, struck a pose and eyed him seductively through the cascading fire. "How could I sell the kind of products I do if I had a boyish figure?"

"How much, and where do I run to buy it?"

"To your nearest Rawley outlet. And while you're at it, pick up some of their men's cologne, as well. I go mad over men who use Midnight Musk Oil. The scent that compliments his body to the nth degree," she intoned in a sultry voice.

"Liz'beth, if you go on like this, I'm never going to get out of here. And I badly want to see you in that bathing suit."

"And you?" she teased, her eyes sparkling. "Will you be putting on abbreviated trunks?"

"I'll swim in the nude, if you like," he offered innocently.

She shook her head calmly, though she was feeling far from calm. He had definitely won the round and her flush told him so.

"Or I could combine the two by hunting up a loincloth," he went on, patently enjoying himself now.

"I think we've talked this particular subject to death," she mumbled, all but burying her head in her suitcase as she hunted for the two tiny strips of cloth that claimed to be a bathing suit. "So if you don't mind, I'll change now."

"I don't mind in the least."

She glanced up, hoping her face looked as composed as she wanted it to be. "Then kindly leave."

"Do you know something, Liz'beth? In many ways you're rather quaint." He smiled. "Almost prudish, in fact, though you try your damnedest to hide it."

"Why?" she demanded. "Because I won't strip in front of you? You must be out of your mind."

He shook his head. "But there are all sorts of little give-aways. I'm not objecting, mind you. It just surprises the hell out fo me. I expected you to have become blasé and diamond hard."

And he was supposed to believe that still. "Nobody remains Snow White in this day and age, Logan," she told him firmly.

He nodded. "Snow White you're not. High fashion wouldn't tolerate the look, but you're a fairly conservative lady, Elizabeth, for all that."

She had found the bikini and she now held up the bits of cloth. "In that case, maybe I'd better not wear this, after all. Grandmother would be shocked."

"Of course, there are two sides to every story," Logan said, backing his way out of the room. "I'll wait for you downstairs. Be quick."

"Logan, wait!" Elizabeth called out to him as he walked through the bathroom. "I just remembered. I don't have any riding boots."

He came back into the room. "What kind of boots do you have?"

"None. Oh, wait a minute. I did bring some dressy ones that go with this dumb cowgirl getup." She proceeded to open a case that she had not unpacked yet, showing him the black, flat-brimmed cabellero hat that lay on top. Logan came forward with an interested look on his face.

"What have you got there?" he questioned.

"Stupidity," she said, bringing out a white suede bolero vest that was studded with black onyx stones. "I wore it on an assignment once, and was told I could keep it as a bonus. It looks great for a magazine ad, but in real life it's just a bit much. I honestly don't know why I brought it."

"Let me see the rest of the outfit," Logan replied.

She showed him the black silk blouse with full, billowing sleeves gathered at the wrists. Then she pulled out white calfskin pants that didn't allow much movement. "They fit like a glove," she told him, "so I can't very well go riding in them. As I said, the outfit was made for show, not practicality."

Logan looked disappointed. "Then you're saying I'm never going to get to see this on you?"

She looked up with the boots in hand. They too were white, with high heels and black onyx studding. She smiled a little. "Not unless you want to take my picture."

Thoughtfully he fingered the brushed suede pants. "What if I held a jamboree here? Spring roundup is nearly over, and the ranch hands and their families will be wanting to celebrate. You could wear this then, couldn't you?"

"I could, yes." She hid her surprise over his concern about her outfit and where she could wear it. "And I think a jamboree would be fun, but won't it be a lot of work? I'd like to help out and I don't think Elvira would—"

Logan was shaking his head. "Everyone brings a pot of something or other, I supply the drinks, and there will be enough old-time fiddlers to make your head ring. This type of thing goes on at the drop of a hat around here. The men love it because it gives them a reason to get pie-eyed, and the women love it because it gives them a chance to get out of their everyday clothes. Anyway, there's no real work involved. Don't you remember the get-togethers you came to when you used to visit?"

She nodded with a bittersweet smile. Her eyes had been busy following Logan around the lit-up yard, and she could recall the unbridled joy of once being asked to dance by the tall, tawny-eyed cattle baron.

"I think it would be great fun, Logan," she repeated, her voice very soft.

They looked at each other for a long moment across the pile of clothes. Logan spoke first. "I remember the first time James ever brought you over to my place. You were...what? Sixteen, seventeen? The most alluring, blue-eyed jailbait any man would ever lay eyes on. I was scared for my men and scared for myself. I told James not to let you out of his sight."

"But you did ask me to dance," she reminded him.

"I shouldn't have," he said, his voice a little dry now. "It only intensified the fear."

"I'm glad I didn't know how you felt," Elizabeth said, thinking about the quiet naive girl who had only just previously escaped from the close supervision of her grandmother's house. With her wide-eyed view of the world, she would not have appreciated knowing that a thirty-year-old man was feeling sexually stirred by her.

It had taken her two more years to catch up to those feelings. And in a way, since that night in the barn with Logan, she had been running away from such unmanageable feelings ever since. Better not to fall too deeply in love. Better not to allow your body to hold sway over your mind had been her unconscious credo. Elizabeth was convinced that passionate, emotional women always got hurt. They invariably became victims of their own vulnerability.

She looked up and saw that he was questioning her with his eyes. She shrugged. "It seems so distant to me," she lied, breaking the mood that held him there.

Immediately his expression closed to her. "I'll go see if I can hunt up some less spectacular boots for you. We usually have all shapes and sizes on hand for out-of-town visitors. What size do you wear?"

"Six and a half," she replied. "And I'd prefer a two-inch heel."

He smiled patiently. "Any particular color?"

"No—but good quality leather would be nice."

"Naturally. You know, Elizabeth, I didn't mean to intimate that I own a shoe shop."

She waved him away. "Just do the best you can, then."

"That wart's going to grow on your nose anytime now, lady."

"Madman. It wouldn't dare."

FEED MILLS, weigh stations and the rounded-up herds of cattle greeted her vision from the bluff of a foothill. The smell of branding wafted on the breeze, causing her horse to whicker, while the distant clanging of a dinner bell drew her eyes to a chuck wagon, surrounded by dotlike figures of men. Elizabeth felt as though she were looking down on a movie set of the old West.

The most striking visual appeal of the wild regions of the valley land could be found here, for the range property had been charted out amid cobalt-blue lakes, lush grazing meadows, thundering cateracts and sheer mountain faces. Because the land embraced both prairie and mountain, it was alive with diverse plants and animals. The lowlands were sprinkled with pasqueflowers, wild roses, moss phlox and geraniums of brilliant pinks and purples, and during their ride into the high country, she had seen white-tailed deer, prey of cougars and coyotes, moving cautiously across open meadows.

With a word and nudge of his boots, Logan directed his spirited mount to still-higher ground; Elizabeth's horse passively followed the huge stallion.

The grasses gave way to a carpet of lichens and mosses, and the riders entered a cool forest of spruce and larch. Following a pattern of trunk roads, they eventually reached a clearing where a glacial waterfall created a pool, sparkling clear and inviting.

"Behold, ye old swimming hole," Logan said, as he dismounted and came to help Elizabeth.

Elizabeth was gazing around, her expression radiant. "Logan," she almost whispered, "is this paradise?" Adding to the beauty of the scene was an abundance of wild flowers and lacy green ferns.

"I thought you might like it," he said softly.

Grasping his proffered hand, Elizabeth swung her leg around to the front of the saddle and winced and moaned with the movement.

"Good grief," she exclaimed, when Logan had set her safely on her feet. "How did all that stiffness creep up on me?"

"All comes from being a tenderfoot."

"I thought I was a 'greenhorn,'" she said, taking a few careful steps.

"Naw...you're too pretty for a greenhorn."

She made it to the bank of the pool and eased herself down on a flat rock. "This will be perfect for sunbathing," she said, patting the ready-made platform.

Logan unsaddled both horses, then led them to a shady nook on the other side of the pond. He tied them loosely so they would be able to drink.

"Don't forget our lunch," she called to him. "We can eat on this rock, too."

Her eyes danced and sparkled as he closed in on her, obligingly carrying the haversack of food. "Having fun, are you?" he murmured, his expression amused.

"Yes." She put her hands to her hair and fluffed it up and away from her perspiring face. "And I can't decide whether to swim and die of starvation in the meantime or to eat and expire from the heat."

He dropped the haversack in her lap. "Well, whichever way you do it, you're setting the table."

She shrugged as she opened the haversack. "Fine. I hope Elvira included a tablecloth—a red checkered one. There's just something about a red checkered tablecloth."

"Well?" Logan said, watching her frown begin.

"There's only a couple of ugly brown mats in here."

He hunkered down beside her. "Try not to take it so hard."

She raised her eyes to him. "Who ever heard of a picnic without a checkered tablecloth to eat it on?"

"I'll severely reprimand Elvira about this."

"You think it's all a big joke, don't you? Well, this happens to be the first real picnic I've been on in years. I had this picture of exactly how it would be. You did your part by bringing me to this absolutely perfect spot, but...Logan?"

"Yes?" He smiled and stretched out beside her.

"Do you suppose next time I could fix the lunch?"

"Of course. You don't even need to ask."

She grimaced a little at that, then said, "I'll have to go down to Kate's store first, though."

"To get a tablecloth?" Logan shook his head. "Don't bother. Elvira has all shapes and patterns put away somewhere."

Elizabeth gave him a tiny smile. "I want to get a pair of those beautiful, handmade mocassin slippers that she wears as well. Kate would sell those, wouldn't she?"

"Sure," Logan confirmed, watching as Elizabeth placed the haversack in the shade of the jutting rock. "You decided to swim first, I take it?"

Elizabeth nodded and began to undo her blouse. "I feel too grimy to eat, and I think the water might help to limber me up, as well."

"I should warn you about that water," Logan said lazily, watching her movements. "It comes from a subterranean lake inside the mountain and it's frozen for most of the year. So you're in for a shock, I'm afraid."

Undeterred, Elizabeth discarded her blouse. "I'll ease in carefully, then. Aren't you coming in?"

"I'll just watch," he said, his eyes drifting over her scantily clad breasts.

Elizabeth, seeing his admiring gaze, looked down to make sure she was relatively decent. The bra top showed a great deal of cleavage, and the jersey material outlined her nipples a little too clearly for this kind of close perusal. Before her Rawley Girl days, she had modeled for a swimwear company, and this suit in particular had created a press sensation under the advertiser's heading of Riviera Days and Nights. It was this campaign, in fact, that had prompted the Rawley people to incline their heads her way.

Posing in the suit for a camera, however, now seemed an awful lot easier than having Logan's eyes trained on her. She decided his own completely clothed state was part of the problem.

"Come on, Logan, I insist you join me. You did say you would go along with my every whim."

"I did, didn't I? Very well, Liz'beth, but I'll let you test the water for me first."

"Coward," she replied, aiming a slight frown at him.

She slid off her boots and jeans with some effort, keeping her face turned slightly away from Logan. By not looking directly at her audience, Elizabeth knew she could avoid feeling self-conscious—death to a career in modeling.

Standing proudly erect, she scooped her hair up in a twist on the top of her head, then reached down to pluck one of the two laces from the hipline of the suit. She caught Logan's raised eyebrow as she tied her hair with it.

"Isn't that a little like the straw that broke the camel's back?" Logan muttered, obviously surprised that the minuscule bottom portion of the aqua-colored suit was still intact.

Elizabeth smiled, enjoying the warm sensations his eyes were causing in her body.

"Do women actually wear suits like that on a public beach?" Logan asked, slowly rising to his feet.

Elizabeth dipped a toe in the water, conscious that he was beginning to undo his shirt. "They do if they have good enough figures. In fact, there are a lot of topless beaches around these days, Logan. You really ought to try and find the time to do some traveling. You may find it well worth your while."

"I have done quite a bit of traveling, though it's usually with the Canadian Cattlemen's Association," he returned. "And to date there have been no conventions held on topless beaches. So tell me, Elizabeth, would you go topless on these beaches?"

She caught sight of his bare chest and then turned quickly back to the water. "Yes, I have gone topless on one or two occasions. You stand out like a sore thumb if you don't."

"I wish you had sent me a postcard," he intoned softly.

Her peripheral vision caught the movement of his hands on his belt buckle, making her aware of the charged atmosphere that she had been trying to ignore. How ridiculous, she thought, to panic simply because Logan was going to remove his pants to go swimming. How ridiculous to view this whole scene as though it were a slow-motion, highly provocative, striptease. And yet that's exactly how it felt.

"You aren't wearing that loincloth, are you, Logan?" she had to ask before looking at him.

She heard him chuckle. "And if I was?"

She turned, relieved to see that he was only in the process of pulling off his boots. An arrow of chest hair drew her attention to the loosened waist of his jeans.

"I think I'll have to call you a fraud." She eyed his chest with hard-won composure. "Indians are supposed to be pretty hairless, aren't they?"

His grin widened. "Are they?"

"That's what I've heard."

"Well, I think there were a couple of hairy apes on my father's side."

"And no doubt you feel you've hit on the happy medium?"

"I dunno." He looked up at her with his thumbs hooked in a readying position at the hips of his jeans. "Ready, Liz'beth?"

"For what?" she asked succinctly.

"For the fact that I wasn't really planning on swimming. Do I look the sort of man who'd have Speedo trunks on hand?"

She stared at him. "But you were the one who suggested..."

He shook his head. "I told you about a dandy swimming hole, and asked if you could get a bathing suit on under those designer jeans of yours. I didn't say a thing about me swimming."

Her gaze became flinty. "You knew I was expecting you to swim."

He acknowledged that with a shrug. "The few times I've been here, I've dived in baby naked. It's pretty private, so a bathing suit never was a priority."

Against her will, her eyes were drawn to the area where his fly was partially undone. "Well, surely you're wearing something?"

He nodded. "Wet cotton is pretty revealing, but I don't mind if you don't."

She shook her head quickly. The fact that she had briefly glimpsed him naked the night before should have made some difference, she supposed, but it didn't. She had effectively blocked that raw masculine sight of him out of her mind, and she had no wish to aid that particular imagery now.

"Then I suggest you stay exactly as you are," she told him.

"Why don't we both strip instead?" he suggested easily.

"And why don't you take a flying leap off a cliff?"

"Come on, Elizabeth, what's a little nakedness between friends? You're halfway there, anyway."

"This," she told him, "is as far as I go."

"You said you've gone topless before."

"You weren't there!"

"Then I affect you in some special way?"

She closed here eyes briefly. "No."

"Prove it. I'll try and be as blasé as the next guy."

"Oh, you will, will you?" she said, her own lips curving just a bit.

"I said I'd try," he qualified.

"I won't have to prepare myself for any sudden lunges?" She raised her eyebrows quizzically.

He crossed his heart and hoped to die. "Have fun, Liz'beth." His voice was decidedly husky. Sitting on the rock cross-legged he continued to coax. "Now I can't even lunge, so you can sit beside me."

She shook her head. "I don't trust you."

He looked up at the sun. "Lie down beside me, then. I'm only concerned that you get an all-over tan."

"How touching. Would you mind terribly if I cooled off in the water first?"

"Suit yourself. But I did warn you about that water."

She turned back to the sparkling clarity of the pond. Her toe had just barely passed the test, so she sat down and carefully eased her legs into the water. Gritting her teeth, she said,

"Why, it's beautiful! Can't you swim, Logan? Is that what this is really all about?"

"You're just trying to get me to take my pants off, after all."

Goose bumps covered her flesh and her legs went numb, and Elizabeth knew there was absolutely no way she could submerge herself in such icy water. "Damn," she said, withdrawing her legs.

"Told ya," he drawled.

Cupping some water in her hand she threw it at him; he raised his arm in front of his face belatedly. "If there's anything I can't stand it's a smartass," she told him.

His face dripping, he said, "Now Elizabeth, you really shouldn't have done that. You don't really want me to throw you in that pond, do you?"

"No." She stared at him, sincerely hoping that he'd been joking. "I...I didn't mean to splash you so much, Logan. I just thought a few drops might be refreshing."

"You did, huh?" He uncrossed his legs slowly.

On the outcrop, Elizabeth was caught firmly between the water and Logan, who looked like he was preparing to advance on her. "Please don't, Logan," she said, the plea in her voice very real.

He held out his hand to her and said softly, "Come here, Elizabeth."

The subtle change in his manner struck her as trickery, so she shook her head.

"Liz'beth," he said patiently. "I wouldn't dream of throwing you in that icy water."

She might have believed him if he had not started walking the few steps toward her.

She felt cornered and determined not to end up in the ice-cold pond, so she quickly offered him a distraction—one that was guaranteed to stop him in his tracks. With two quick tugs, the top of her string bikini fell into her hand, and Logan immediately halted.

She watched his eyes hungrily roam her breasts. She heard his quick intake of breath, his slow exhalation and then she was meeting the dark embers of his eyes.

He shook his head a little. "Stealing a man's breath away is a hell of a good defense." His eyes dropped to her breasts again, as if magnetically drawn to their perfect symmetry. He closed his eyes.

Elizabeth's knees felt weak, and she shivered involuntarily as his eyes slowly opened. She wanted his touch, wanted his strong arms around her, wanted his warmth and his kisses. But she stood as she was—stiff and still, hardly daring to breathe—afraid of the yearning need that was filling her. If he touched her now he would awaken the very core of her, that part of her she was trying to keep under lock and key.

"Logan," she said, striving to keep the breathlessness out of her voice. "Don't..." She crossed her arms and covered each breast with a hand. "That is, you look as though you're about to lunge. And...you did promise."

He looked enviously at her hands. "All right," he said after a long moment, exhaling a heavy breath. "I give up, Liz'beth. Where is it?"

"What are you talking about?"

"The flaw. The birthmark, the wart, the freckle, for pity sake. Where are you hiding it? Your breasts, I might add, are sculptured art objects."

Taken a little aback, she thought hard, trying valiantly to accommodate. It seemed so important to him. "Well, as a matter of fact, I do have a few freckles," she told him.

"Where?" he demanded.

She turned around and presented her back to him. "There. On my shoulders."

She heard him step closer and then she felt his eyes boring into her. "You have no freckles," he told her flatly.

She frowned. "Logan, I'm a redhead. There must be a few freckles. I used to have lots of them."

"Well, they flew the coop, then."

She was about to turn around, but just before she made the move, she felt the warm touch of his lips on one sun-warmed shoulder, then his hand came to settle there. "But I forgive you," he murmured.

Her nerve endings jumped as she responded to his touch. Her breath seemed to catch and lodge in her throat.

"I won't tell you that your skin has the flawless texture of satin," he said softly. "Because you've heard it all before." His hands began to smooth and caress her shoulders, moving upward toward her nape. "And I won't tell you that your hair is a fragrant dark flame that enchants me every time you move your head." His fingers touched the tendrils that had escaped the upswept fastening. "Because you've heard all that before, too..."

With her eyes closed and her head falling forward with the soothing manipulation of his caressing fingers, Elizabeth allowed her breath to escape in a long exhalation, hoping he wouldn't hear.

"And your breasts," he went on. "Does a man dare comment there, too? What have other men told you about your breasts, Elizabeth?"

Her nipples began to harden under her palms, in direct response to the husky timbre of his words. She wondered if he had any knowledge of what he was doing to her, of how vibrantly she was responding to him. She cared nothing of other men—what they saw in her or how they reacted to her. She wanted only to be special for Logan...for Logan to think her beautiful and desirable. She had always wanted that.

"Tell me, sweetheart," he murmured, his hands retracking now, moving over each slim shoulder and down her arms, while he kissed the hollow of a shoulder that he had left behind.

As he embraced her from behind, his hands covered hers. "Do they tell you they look as though they've never been touched?" he breathed against her throat. "As though their perfect roundness has never been disturbed?"

Elizabeth was torturing herself with her attempt at steady breathing, but when his palms pressed against her hands, she knew there was no way she could maintain control. Her heart was beating furiously beneath her palm as her breathing quickened audibly, and she knew that Logan must finally be aware of it, too.

His fingers curled around hers, decreasing the pressure he had caused until her own palms brushed softly against the hardened tips of her breasts. But the circular manipulation was still all his.

Now her head fell back against his shoulder, her breasts jutting forward toward the source of her pleasure.

"And your nipples," he went on, his voice thick. "Did you know that dusky pink was my favorite color, Liz'beth?"

"Logan," she protested softly, self-conscious in the act they were performing together. But she had also become subject to the drowning need she had tried to fight against. The need that was always there, just below the surface whenever she was with him. "Please don't," she said, not knowing if she meant it or not.

He then brought her hands down to her side, and she knew his eyes were on the hardened points they had left behind.

She felt an unbearable ache growing within her when his hands moved to her waist, his splayed fingers touching her naked belly, causing her muscles to contract. Elizabeth closed her eyes as his hands covered her rib cage, stopping their slow upward glide when the curve of his thumb and forefinger neatly framed each of her breasts.

She leaned back against him then, turning her face to meet the lips that had been grazing her cheek. Their mouths melted together for endless moments, and then Elizabeth was moaning softly when his thumbs at last began to stroke her nipples, brushing slowly back and forth to create an ecstatic friction.

He shifted and she turned in his arms, and then she was being kissed and held as he stroked her from breast to shoulder, shoulder to thigh, his hands molding her slimness to him, his mouth branding her as his.

"Logan, Logan," she breathed, clutching at him now. She needed to lie down, to be touched and held and cradled against him. Her mouth became aggressive on his, her hands moved up to cup his hard jaw, to stroke his cheek, and then her hands clasped his head, her fingers moving against his scalp.

When at last their mouths parted, Logan drew back to see her tortured expression. Gently kissing her brow and her cheek, her chin and her nose, he murmured, "This hard rock we're standing on has got to go."

She nodded. Her legs felt as though they would no longer support her. She closed her eyes as he swung her into his arms, his head lowering to kiss the tempting mounds of her breasts before he began to walk back across the rocky surface to the grassy area beyond.

They were in a sun-dotted shuttered world of trees and sheer mountain flank—a perfect spot for making love, except for one thing. The grasses, Logan noted, were heavily strewn with dandelions and nettles, so he was forced to search for another spot on which to place his beautiful weak-kneed burden.

A burden who was currently stirring, with a little line of concern forming on her brow. He leaned down to kiss it away.

"Where are you taking me?"

"Shh. Close your eyes," he instructed.

"Logan," she said, staring at him again, the heavy-lidded look fast fading. "I think you'd better put me down."

Logan did the best thing he could under the circumstances—he lowered her into a sitting position on a moss-strewn rocky ledge that projected from the mountain at about hip level, so her face was even with his. He moved his body between her knees and began kissing her, bringing his hands to rest on either side of her head.

He kissed her long and hard, until she was breathless and her eyes became smoky with desire. Only...

Logan frowned a little, looking at her heavily lashed eyes as she blinked them farther open. Their vivid blue color seemed a little at odds with the depths of the smoking embers within.

"What is it?" she asked, her voice husky and warm. She felt bereft without the moist heat of his seeking mouth.

He shook his head a little. "I don't know quite what... Something about your eyes, Liz'beth. They're...too blue."

"Oh," Elizabeth shrugged, bringing her hands up to his shoulders, "those are just my contacts. They're tinted."

With the movement of her body, his gaze had wandered to her breasts. But on completion of her statement, his eyes flew to hers.

"What?" he said, as if he hadn't heard her correctly.

She looked at his mouth with sweet impatience. "I said my contacts are tinted."

"You wear contacts?"

"Yes." She blinked and smiled at him.

Logan felt his heart flip over in his chest. "You...have bad eyesight?" he asked carefully.

She nodded. "Everything's blurry around the edges if I don't wear them."

He leaned forward to kiss her nose—a warm, gentle, funny little kiss that tickled her. "In other words, gorgeous Liz, you're as blind as a bat?" He sounded hopeful.

"Well, I wouldn't go that far, but it is pretty bad," she said obligingly. "I may have to wear fairly strong glasses in the future."

"You mean that?"

Again she nodded, though she felt compelled to say, in view of his broadening smile, "It's hardly anything to feel happy about, is it? I mean, bad eyesight is no joke."

"I know that," he said, becoming appropriately subdued. "And anyway...I have this uneasy feeling that you'll suit glasses. In fact, I would have felt much better about a wart because there would be no real hardship involved there." He peered at her. "Can you see me clearly now?"

Elizabeth tried desperately not to laugh. Logan, she thought, was looking *clearly* devastating—masculinity at its best. He looked roguishly sexy with his fuzzy bronzed chest and his slightly unbuttoned jeans, his hair tousled forward on his brow just a bit and this endearing look of peering concern.

Her rekindled needs had not left her, and she was aware of what she was doing when she sat a little straighter and released her bottom lip to say, "Yes—perfectly. Can you see me?"

Which effectively marked the end of light banter or medical concern on Logan's part. She shook her head as he murmured, "Temptress," but then her lips parted at the touch of his mouth on her breast. Her head fell back as his mouth closed over a nipple, tonguing it and sucking it with such expertise that the world tipped and swayed. He continued to make love to her with his lips and his hands, containing his own rising need against the warmth of her parted thighs.

He stroked her back, fitting his hands into the curve of her waist and the swell of her hips as he brought her nipples to quivering tautness. Only then did his lips move lower, whispering to her to lean back against the mossy mountain flank.

Her senses swimming, she did as he asked and immediately felt the searing warmth of his mouth at her waist, the moist tip of his tongue at her navel.

She protested softly when she felt a soft tug at her hip, and then squirmed when she felt the other side of her bikini bottom give way, as well.

"Liz'beth," he murmured, bringing his lips back to her waist, "don't you want me to?"

"I...I do want you, Logan," she said, for denying it to him or herself would have been useless. Every inch of her flesh responded to his merest touch and he knew that as well as she.

"But on your terms, hmm?" he murmured, burying his face in her neck.

Her fingers trailed down his back to the waist of his jeans, and she closed her eyes when his warm breath moved to her ear, igniting sensations that made her tremble.

"I want to take you right now," he said urgently. "But is that what you want?"

Her response was to tighten her legs around him—a response that made him groan.

She felt him tug on the triangular front of her bikini bottoms, and then she was lifting her hips to help, vibrantly conscious of the parted position of her legs. He tossed the bikini briefs aside, and then he was drawing back, his palms cupping each knee as he took in this new sight of her.

"Logan..." she protested softly, despite the erotic feelings that were flashing through her. His eyes met hers with a smoldering look, and then he was working at his pants, pushing them down, stepping out of them with no wasted movements. She felt hurried and desperate, too, when he moved back into her waiting warmth, his hard, throbbing desire nudging against her for entrance.

Before Charles there had been a couple of men, based more on the need to experiment than on sexual excitement, but the moment Logan united his body with hers, she realized just how meaningless those encounters had been. She knew, too, that she could never experience this kind of suspended joy with Charles, no matter how perfectly suited to her she had thought him. She had wanted a man who was not too possessive or too time-consuming, and quite simply, Charles had filled the bill, for she'd had no inclination for the kind of relationship that could turn a woman into a quivering mass of vulnerability, subject to the dictates of love.

But Logan was peeling away her facade layer by layer, and when he lifted her to him for deeper penetration, she felt as though he had broken through the dam of her feelings, and now great waves needed to come rushing through.

When the first raindrop fell, Logan spared a moment to look up at an overcast sky, and he cursed inwardly, but for Elizabeth there was no awareness beyond Logan and what he could do for her. She wrapped her limbs tightly around him, taking him deep inside her by degrees as she kissed him and held to him with an urgency that no past experiences had ever prepared her for.

Logan's groan was audible, and it had nothing to do with the dime-size drops that were now spattering his back. He hugged her to him, leaning forward to shield her, and then there was nothing but the hard-driving need she had aroused and demanded of him.

He had meant to ask her about protection, in view of the lukewarm relationship she had described concerning Charles Durney. There was, he felt, a strong possibility that Elizabeth was not on the pill. He cursed himself for not being better prepared...for not even thinking about this aspect of things until it was too late. He was remembering what Elizabeth had said about children and people's cruelty and choices. But mostly he was thinking about the simple horror she would feel if he made her pregnant.

But all these thoughts fled the moment he felt the moist receptiveness of her woman's body. He would never have believed she could be so ready for him without the preliminaries he had intended to lavish on her. Her womanliness awed him, and he kissed her voraciously, his tongue seeking out the soft, throaty sounds that she was, as yet, attempting to keep back from him.

He whispered to her and encouraged her as the skies opened in earnest. A crack of thunder heralding the deluge and muffled Elizabeth's building cries as she gave herself up to the driving rhythm of his body.

The warm rain beat against them, mixed with the tears that had begun to stream down Elizabeth's face as she gasped and moaned and clung to him in an explosive, blinding release. To her it seemed that the storm and their passion were one, and that each crack of thunder marked an indelible change in the universe. And in the far-flung fragments of that universe she was so small a part. Her throat ached and her heart ached, because now she knew she belonged body and soul to Logan. There was no going back.

7

COLD, SHIVERING, HUNGRY and dressed in sodden clothes, Elizabeth was not looking her best. Rivulets of mascara created by the rain and by her tears had left black smudges beneath her eyes, which Logan was trying to wipe away. The rain had stopped, but the world remained dreary and damp, much like the desolate waiflike creature, standing passively under Logan's frowning regard.

"You have to speak to me sooner or later, you know," he said, looking none too happy himself in the aftermath. "I asked you a simple question, I think. Are you or are you not on the Pill?"

"Isn't it a little late to be asking?" she said, speaking her very first words. Her voice, however, was flat and lifeless.

"That isn't an answer," he said, his jaw tautening as his thumb left her face. His patience was thinning, for it seemed to him she should realize how important this was. Even disregarding any other considerations, pregnancy and a career like hers did not go together. He was feeling guilty and angry with himself, and he supposed he wasn't helping the situation by badgering her, but he felt he needed to know.

Then, too, her unnatural silence and her robotlike passivity were beginning to irk him—making him feel unaccountably guilty, as well. He had held her and kissed her and then had to dress her in that rag-doll state, which had not been easy. He had asked if he had hurt her, and she had shaken her head no. He had asked if she needed something to eat, and again she had merely shaken her head. By the time he had asked her about the Pill, he was trying to refrain from shaking her, for she was making him feel as though he had committed some unmentionable crime. Instead, however, he found himself wiping the smudges from beneath those large, expressive eyes.

Only they weren't telling him anything now.

"Then, no," she said, her voice still as lifeless as her eyes. "I'm not on the Pill, and I don't wear a diaphragm, either. But try not to worry, Logan—it's the wrong time of month. Or the right—depending on your point of view. Does that put your mind at ease?"

"More important, I would think it would put yours at ease. Next time I'll take the responsibility, though."

"Next time?" She looked only curious.

Logan sensed—strongly—that this was no time to talk about the next time. Desire, however, even now, was flickering within, as was tenderness and concern, but she seemed in no mood for any of it. He tried to contain his frustration, his strong urge to take her into the protection of his arms.

"All right. We won't talk about next time. Do you want to go home now?"

"Home?" Once again she looked mildly curious.

Logan carefully unclamped his jaw. "No, Liz. Not back to Toronto. Not yet. Not on your life. I was referring to my home. And in this instance I don't mean the wide-open spaces."

"Okay," she said.

"Dammit, Elizabeth," Logan finally exploded softly. "What's with you? Tell me what in hell I've done! If you're feeling guilty over what's-his-name, I can accept that! I hate it, but I can understand how you might be feeling if you're as serious about him as you claim. I happen to think it's a pretty strange relationship, but I guess I don't have the right to judge."

"No, Logan," she said simply, passively, obligingly. "You don't."

"I give up," he muttered, taking hold of her hand and leading her to the horses. "I can't talk to you when you're like this. 'Like this'—I don't even know what 'this' is. If you were a virgin, and I was a rapist, then I'd say you were in a state of shock. But you aren't, and I'm not, and what's-his-name is no good at it, so I'm at a loss, sweetheart. I thought you enjoyed yourself as much as I did, but I guess I was wrong."

"No, Logan," she said. "You weren't wrong." She collided with his back when he stopped in his tracks. Turning to her, holding her by the shoulders, he looked into her eyes. "Are you telling me that you liked what happened between us?"

"I liked having sex with you," she ventured. Seeing one's world explode into so many useless fragments was something else entirely. It was an irretrievable happening. It was unchangeable. She had become totally her mother's daughter, her mind and soul and body subject to the dictates of the man who had so recently made her his. She considered it a cruel and heartless fate, saw herself drifting back to her smashed world and fumbling with the tiny pieces as she tried to fit them together—tried to find some satisfaction in the cracked mosaic that would hereafter be her life. Her only hope was that he would not want to send her back yet. She would need more memories to see her through. She would need to close her eyes and think of Logan when any other man ever held her. She would need to do this in order to create the illusion of a full life.

So, no. She did not like what had happened to her, but she knew she would drink at the well until it ran dry—until Logan didn't want her anymore.

"You like having sex with me?" Logan repeated, not above treating himself to a double dose of those provocative words. He gave up then and took her into his arms, whether she was disposed at the moment or not. Against her ear he murmured, "Elizabeth, my darling, I love having sex with you. Only next time it's going to be in a soft, warm bed, and I'm going to check for leaks in the ceiling. It was beautiful making love to you in the storm, but I don't think my back could stand an encore. You wore me out, love," he said, nuzzling her damp neck and warming it with his whispered words.

Despite her utter dishevelment, Elizabeth found herself easily rising to the sensual occasion. Though she still shivered outwardly, inside a low fire was being gently blown into licks of flickering flame. She turned her face to meet his seeking mouth, and then her arms moved up to wrap themselves around his neck and shoulders as she gave herself up to the luxury of his warm and passionate kiss.

When he finally withdrew his lips, his breathing was raspy, and his desire was full and hard against her stomach. "Let's go home," he whispered hoarsely, "and lock the door on the world."

Both Red and her father were waiting in the yard when she and Logan rode up. As he helped her dismount near the corral gate, Red walked up to take charge of the horse, Steady Joe. She met the look in Red's eyes with a flush of awareness, for she knew her appearance was speaking a thousand words. Her hair was hanging in long strings, and her shirt and jeans looked as though they had lain in the mud, which of course they had.

"Hi, Elizabeth," Red said, the sensual knowledge in his eyes belying his friendly greeting.

"Hello, Red," Elizabeth greeted him, wishing she felt less self-conscious. "How have you been?"

"Real good." Turning in Logan's direction for a moment. He watched as the taller man unlatched the gate to bring the horses through. "A lot better since catching sight of you, though," he added quietly.

Elizabeth, too, found herself glancing a little furtively at Logan, wondering if he had caught Red's remark and whether

he would attach any particular significance to it. She knew
that if Kate and Logan hadn't told her about Red's feelings
toward her, she herself would have thought nothing of the
softly worded comment. As it was, though, she sensed
something other than friendliness in his words. She strove for
a light reply.

"Well, as you can see, I am a sight. Logan and I got caught
in the storm."

"So I gathered." Red's eyes drifted over her once again.

"Unsaddle the horses, will you, Red?" Logan said abruptly as he came back to Elizabeth. "And then have Jake give
them a good rubdown."

"Sure, boss."

At that moment James joined them by the fence. "Good
grief," he said mildly, looking at Logan and Elizabeth. "What
did you do? Get caught in a mud slide?"

Elizabeth could feel a furious blush building in her cheeks
as she waited for Logan to come up with some kind of response. She could think of nothing to say that would mini-
mize the obvious.

"Never mind about us, James," Logan came through,
smoothly changing the subject. "What about you? Are you
sure you don't want to stick around here for a few more days?
You told me to call Red back, so I did. But I can always send
him over to your place again."

Logan's expression told Elizabeth that he would like to do
just that. His gaze was fixed steadily on his foreman as Red
led Elizabeth's mount past them.

"No. Thanks anyway, Logan. Sweetwater's where I belong and Red is needed here." James smiled. "That way you'll
be able to take good care of my daughter. Although—" James
looked down at her "—I can't say you've been doing a very
good job so far. Honey," he said to Elizabeth, "You look like
something the cat dragged in. You didn't fall off that horse,
did you?"

"I..." Elizabeth glanced up at Logan a little helplessly. "Actually, James, I was about to go swimming when the storm hit, so I just left my clothes where I dropped them."

By now James appeared to be wishing he hadn't asked. His reply, however, resurrected Elizabeth's composure. "Oh, well, that explains it." On a quieter note, he said, "And I'm glad you changed your mind about returning to Toronto tonight. I'll be hoping to see you at Sweetwater often, Liz...I guess Logan won't mind bringing you."

"You can count on that," Logan said, placing his arm around Elizabeth's shoulders. "In fact, we'll both come along with you tonight, if you like. Elizabeth said you were going to take in some kind of meeting?"

"It will be some meeting, all right," James agreed, looking pained. "But a little bitter medicine never hurt anybody."

"Well, we'll make sure you get there safe and sound," Logan said. "I'll take Elizabeth out to dinner while you're confessing your sins. All right?" he said, looking down at her upturned face.

Though the suggestion was unexpected, Elizabeth was readily agreeable. She was also strongly conscious of the united front they were presenting to James and Red. It was for the latter man, Elizabeth suspected, that Logan was making this proprietary show.

When they entered the house together, Logan steered her directly into the kitchen. Raiding the refrigerator with Logan was an unexpected treat. With him by her side, and Elvira resting in her downstairs room, Elizabeth felt no qualms about walking on the new cushion floor. Between the two of them, Elizabeth supposed they devoured every leftover in sight, their soggy picnic lunch having been discarded.

As they were sharing the last chicken leg, Logan backed her up against the fridge and said, "I think I ought to eat the rest, because otherwise you'll get too hippy."

"Hippie?" she questioned. "As in flower child?"

He looked down at her, his eyes both admiring and possessive. "No." His free hand moved down to stroke the definite curve of her hips. "As in something a man can really grab hold of."

With his touch and his words, the memory of their outdoor passion flooded her, and she felt her knees grow weak as his gaze lifted to make contact with hers.

"And you wouldn't like that?" she inquired softly.

He threw the chicken leg over his shoulder, and a slightly shocked Elizabeth watched it land on the clean floor.

"I would love it," he murmured, both hands anchored firmly now on each hip as he brought her against him, "but I don't think the fashion mags would. Do you?"

Her eyelids drooped as her mouth parted for him.

"Your lips are greasy," he murmured.

"So are yours," she said, opening her eyes. "Logan...this may not be the moment for it...but I'd like you to know all the same. I can cook chicken that's just as good as Elvira's"

He gave her a crooked smile. "You're telling me you can cook?"

"I'm telling you that I like to cook—strange as that may seem."

He shook his head. "You don't belong in a kitchen, Elizabeth. Any man who would put you there deserves to be shot."

"But doesn't it count that I don't mind?"

"Nope. Liz'beth, don't try and fight what you are. 'Cause personally—" he brushed her lips with his "—I wouldn't have you any other way."

"And what way is that?" she asked carefully. "Playmate of the month?"

"Cover girl—through and through," he substituted, meeting her look and understanding it.

She could find no real fault with his reply. Still, she felt her definition suited the circumstance better.

"Except right now," he mused with a frown, looking at her hair.

"I realize I'm a mess, Logan," she retorted. "But it was your idea that we grab something to eat first."

"Because I knew you'd collapse if we didn't," he said, taking her hand. "Come on, we're going to wash your hair."

"We?"

"You don't mind if I run my fingers through your hair, do you?"

"Logan, wait," she said when they were halfway across the room. "We have to pick up that chicken leg."

"I can't wait—the shower is beckoning, Liz'beth."

Despite the heady awareness that statement engendered, Elizabeth stooped to pick up the chicken leg, saying, "Get me a wet cloth, please."

"Leave it," Logan instructed, just as Elvira entered the room.

Elizabeth rose slowly, guilt written all over her face. Elvira's eyes went to the chicken leg and then down to the grease spot on the floor. To Logan, she said, as though Elizabeth were not present, "Why didn't you call me to prepare something for you?"

"We managed fine on our own, Elvira," Logan assured her. "Just a little food droppage here."

"That's to be expected," Elvira said, with a brief glance at Elizabeth. To Logan she said, "Henry Carruthers and his son have just driven up with a horse trailer. I thought you'd be wanting to know."

Logan slapped his hand to his brow. "Dadblastit." He turned to Elizabeth. "I forgot that Carruthers said he'd bring him today. Is James still here?" he asked Elvira.

The Indian woman shook her head. "He drove off a short while ago. Said he needed to arrange a sale of one of his mares and a yearling."

"Damn."

"Logan, what's the problem?" Elizabeth asked. "Obviously James plans on giving you that down payment as soon as possible. Can't you keep the horse here for a day or two?"

Logan shook his head. "Of course I can—that isn't the problem. There is no problem, in fact, other than my promise to take the Carruthers boy on a guided tour of the place. He's interested in animal husbandry, and since the horse was supposed to be for him, it seemed the least I could do, so I promised him a *personal* tour," Logan emphasized. "I thought if James were here, he could take over on the horse-breeding end of it if I built him up to the boy enough."

Elizabeth was extremely conscious of Elvira's listening presence. "Well, that's fine, Logan. Really. You shouldn't feel that you have to amuse me, and I'm very grateful on my father's behalf. By all means, please, give the boy his tour. I'm...I'm only sorry you're being put out to this extent for James's sake." She took a deep breath when she was through, not even daring to glance at Elvira.

Logan, looking a little impatient with her, took two steps forward, so he was very close. Placing his hands on either side of her face, he lowered his head and kissed her softly but thoroughly. "I hope to hell I can keep on amusing you," he murmured, when he had slowly released her lips. "But I guess that will have to wait until tonight."

"Logan, please," Elizabeth whispered, her face flushing. "Not in front of Elvira."

"Why not? Elvira doesn't mind if I kiss you," he said loud enough for the woman to hear. "Do you, Elvira?"

"No, Logan." Elvira busied herself wiping the counter.

"Damn right," Logan's eyes never left Elizabeth's face. "When you get ready for dinner tonight," he went on, in that soft, low voice, "wear something sexy and beautiful. I want everyone to know that I've become the luckiest man on earth. Will you do that, sweetheart?"

Elizabeth was incapable of doing anything but nodding. She felt warm and flustered and extremely self-conscious.

Logan left her then, saying "Don't bother with a meal tonight, Elvira. I'm taking Elizabeth into Calgary along with James."

Elvira nodded and then Logan was gone. Elizabeth realized she was still holding the chicken leg.

"Maybe I'd better take that," Elvira said, holding out her hand.

Elizabeth handed it over as though it were stolen goods.

"The garbage container is here," Elvira said, opening a cupboard door below the sink.

"I knew that," Elizabeth said a little defensively.

As Elvira chucked in the remains of the chicken leg, she noticed the varied assortment of bones recently deposited. "So I see. You and Logan must have been very hungry."

"I'm sorry. I hope we've left something for your supper?"

"That is not your worry. Besides, I am a very light eater."

"Well, I'll just clean up this mess on the floor..." Elizabeth said, looking about for a rag.

"No. I'll clean that."

"But there's no reason you should have to."

"It's my job. Please, Miss Jackson, don't concern yourself. I know my place, but if you'll forgive me for saying so, you don't seem to know yours."

Elizabeth stared at the woman for a moment, then her blue eyes took on a definite glint. "Just what do you mean by that, Elvira?"

"Only that you are Logan's guest, but you don't seem willing to be treated accordingly. I have never known one of Logan's guests to come into my kitchen and offer to help cook the meal." Amazingly Elvira smiled at her. "Particularly one as glamorous as you, Miss Jackson."

"I...well, thank you."

"I think perhaps I offended you when I said that high heels leave dents in the floor, but I didn't mean to do that. You will just have to forgive me for feeling a little nervous around you, Miss Jackson, and knowing that it would be best for me to prepare the meal alone."

"You feel nervous around me?"

Elvira nodded. "You are on television. I saw you again just a little while ago in my room. It seems so amazing to walk into another room and see you in person. I try very hard not to stare."

Elizabeth took this in carefully. "You manage that very well," she had to say, thinking of how Elvira tended to make her feel invisible.

"Thank you. I did not wish to make you feel uncomfortable."

"Oh, you didn't. And. . .thank you." Even now, Elvira was looking at a spot past her head.

"Miss Jackson, you have to realize this is quite a treat for all of us who knew you in the past. That hat you wore when you arrived? I have the picture of you wearing that hat on the cover of *Chatelaine*. I have several others, too. I say to Cade, 'You see this beautiful lady? She used to come here every summer as a girl, and every man on this place just couldn't help but fall in love with her. Not just because she was beautiful, but because she had a smile and a wave for everyone.'"

Elizabeth kept looking over her shoulder at the clock, for this was where Elvira's gaze was now centered.

"I told Cade that when you arrived, he was to just help with the luggage and then make himself scarce. No staring, and no speaking unless he was spoken to. I didn't want him to make you feel hounded or ill at ease. He didn't, did he, Miss Jackson?"

Elizabeth quickly shook her head. "No—no, he was a perfect gentleman."

Elvira nodded with satisfaction. "I chewed him out good for not being right on hand for the luggage."

By now Elizabeth was smiling to herself. Who would have thought Elvira would turn out to be a fan?

"You run along, then, and have a good long soak. Getting caught out in the rain can bring on a cold, and the Rawley Girl can't be getting the sniffles. Do you like herbal tea? If so, I could bring a nice hot cup up for you. This is a special blend handed down from my ancestors, and I can guarantee its benefits."

Elizabeth was not an avid tea drinker, but all the same she said, "That would be lovely. And bring a cup up for yourself, too, Elvira. I would like very much to hear all about those ancestors of yours, particularly the grandmother you share with Logan. Tell me, Elvira, was she beautiful?"

With a soft smile Elvira nodded. "Almost as beautiful as you, Miss Jackson. I have pictures of her, as well, so I will bring them up."

An hour later, Elizabeth was looking at the pictures. Her hair wrapped in a thick white towel, she was curled up across from Elvira in the cozy sitting area of the bedroom.

"Elvira...this woman is striking," Elizabeth said. "What was her name?"

"My grandmother was called Moon Glow, for the hour of her birth and because of the soft radiance of her face. Even as an infant, they say, she drew all eyes."

Elizabeth picked up another photo of a much younger woman and said slowly, "This has to be Logan's mother." The resemblance to the grandmother's beautiful, proud features was very strong, although she could easily be taken for a white woman.

"Yes," Elvira said, leaning forward and lifting another picture. "And this is her sister, who, of course, was my mother."

Elizabeth was getting a little confused, for this woman was clearly Indian, with no family resemblance to the subjects in the other photos she had seen.

"You see, it is this way," Elvira went on, seeing Elizabeth's puzzlement. "My grandmother was first married to a man named Joe Hawk, from the reserve. Their daughter was my mother, and she remained on the reserve all her life. But my grandmother had a love for a white man, too, and this white man would not stay away from her even after she married Joe Hawk and had his baby.

"They fought over her, and Joe Hawk was killed. They say it was a fair fight, with both using the same weapons. My grandmother was then taken off the reserve by this white man, who later married her. But he would not accept the child of Joe Hawk. They had a daughter and she looked white, as you can see.

"She grew up to marry the rancher, John Logan, Sr. They say that he did not know her ancestry when he married her, for Moon Glow had by this time gone to her final resting place after being plagued by sickness for many years. I think that she was pining for my mother, whom she had to leave behind on the reserve.

"John Logan, Sr., would not accept his wife's heritage. I do not think he was a bigot so much as he felt duped because she had not told him the truth about things. However, with her child, whom she called Little Logan, in the Indian way, she tried to rectify this mistake by telling him all there was to know.

"When his father died, young Logan went hunting for his heritage, and that is how I come to be here now, along with my son, Cade, and other relatives of mine. My mother was too used to the ways of the reserve and would not come. Now, of course, it is too late. They are all dead, and only Logan and I remain to tell the story of Moon Glow. It is romantic, don't you think?"

Elizabeth was entranced, staring at the picture of Moon Glow and her daughters. "Yes," she agreed. "It isn't often that men fight to the death over a woman." She handed the photos back to Elvira. "I take it then that your mother married on the reserve?"

Elvira nodded. "I am proud to be a full-blooded descendant of the Assiniboine tribe. I took a white name when I left the reserve—my Indian name is too difficult for the white man's tongue. It has too many vowels, you understand, so it does not sound pretty unless you understand the language. And it is not a good one to translate as Moon Glow is. Elvira is pretty, though, don't you think? I heard the name in a song, and I knew I would have it."

"Yes, it's very pretty," Elizabeth agreed again, beginning to understand the soul and substance of the quietly proud woman who was now gazing at the picture of Moon Glow.

"Not as pretty as 'Elizabeth,'" Elvira said, gathering up the treasured photographs. "But that is how it should be. Except I don't like it when people call you Liz because they are too lazy to say the full name. If it were me, I would tell them so plainly and be most annoyed. But I am talking too much, and you look very tired, Miss Jackson. Why don't you take a rest now? I've enjoyed having this tea with you very much, but rest assured I won't presume on your company because of it."

"Elvira, please presume on it as much as you like. And truly, I don't mind in the least if you look at me. Look me right in the eye this minute."

Elvira did, though with apparent difficulty. "Thank you," she said, and then swiftly exited the room.

Elizabeth threw up her hands and uttered a soft laugh as she gazed at the ceiling.

She tried to nap as Elvira had suggested, but found she was too keyed up for anything approaching slumber. Her mind was also on Charles, and the fact that he would be expecting to hear from her by now.

She tossed and turned, conscious that she no longer felt any real allegiance to Charles. Logan had been right in that respect. Without the intimacy of sex, there really was no relationship.

Still, she was very fond of Charles and no doubt owed him a confession of sorts. She hoped he wouldn't be hurt, but other than that, she found herself unable to concern herself with his feelings. He could walk away from her if he liked.

She closed her eyes and relived the time with Logan, feeling the throbbing in her body as a result. Feeling flushed and heated and a little embarrassed with herself, she gave up the bed and started to dress herself in anything that came to hand. She would go for a walk, look in on Dadblastit in the stud barn, see if there were any foals in the stables. Then when she had walked off some of this "energy" she would phone Charles and release him from any obligations he felt toward her. The fact that she would be returning to Toronto in due time didn't really enter into it.

She ran into Hank on her way to the stud barn and waylaid him before he could back off. "You're hurting my feelings, Hank, trying to avoid me this way. I don't look in the least like a glamour girl now, so I don't know why you're acting so silly."

Hank actually blushed. He coughed and stammered and then said, "Heck, Miz Liz, I wasn't trying to avoid you. I jes' thought maybe you was meeting the boss out here. He's been takin' that young greenhorn around abouts."

"Yes, I know that, Hank, but I wasn't planning to meet him. I just wanted to see Dadblastit again, and I was hoping to run into a foal or two." She held out her arm. "Care to escort me?"

Hank scraped his feet. "Yes'm, I shorely would. That old cookhouse can do without me for a spell, I reckon. I'm no good at it, anyway."

"I find that hard to believe, Hank," Elizabeth said when he had gingerly taken her arm. "Why, I bet you can do anything well when you put your mind to it."

"Well, now," Hank said, looking pleased, "I guess I can at that. Like you say, Miz Liz, it's just a case of putting your mind to it. Still, I'll be mighty glad when ol' Ben gets back. Cookin's sissy work, if you ask me."

Elizabeth thought for a moment before she said, "In that case, maybe I could help you out, Hank. I wouldn't go out with the chuck wagon or anything like that, but I could help you with the cooking beforehand. I'm not too bad at it, and maybe between the two of us, it wouldn't be such a chore."

Hank all but stumbled in his tracks. "You mean that, Miz Liz?"

Elizabeth nodded. "Yes, I think I would enjoy it, Hank. Just as long as you weren't expecting Betty Crocker."

"Hell, no. I mean...Heck, Miz Liz, are you sure the boss would go for this? Those men are going to be back from the range any day now, and I can see how they're gonna love this. That's why I'm thinking maybe the boss wouldn't? You know what I mean?"

Hank obviously had been somewhere on hand when she and Logan had ridden up after the storm, Elizabeth thought, with only a slight feeling of embarrassment. Well, she supposed word would get around sooner or later that she and Logan were temporarily a couple, and there wasn't anything she could do about that. Particularly since it seemed to be something that Logan wanted—for people to know they had embarked on a relationship. She remembered what he had said about wearing something sexy for him, and her mind immediately slipped off into a sensual corridor that had nothing to do with Hank.

"Miz Liz?" he questioned, after several moments had passed. "I don't mean to get out of line here, but I feel pretty sure Logan wouldn't like all those men hollering and whistling at you—that's what they'll be doing for shore. The unmarried ones specially."

Elizabeth came back slowly. "Hmm? Oh? Well...I don't think I'd have to serve the men, now would I, Hank? I'll just keep to the kitchen."

"Yep. I guess that would be fine. And I really appreciate it." Hank looked happy and at ease now.

"Good. Then I'll report in the morning. What time, Hank?"

"Five," Hank said blithely.

Elizabeth turned to stare at him. "How about I start with lunch instead?"

"Ten o'clock, then," Hank replied. "We got a lot of bellies to fill up."

"Ten o'clock will be fine," Elizabeth said, hoping she knew what she had let herself in for.

Hank showed her the stall where Dadblastit was housed, and Elizabeth admired the Arabian while stroking his soft nose.

"That horse ain't no pet, and that's a fact," Hank said. "Jake had one hell of a time getting him in here."

"I know," Elizabeth said fondly. "Why do you suppose my father named him Dadblastit?"

"Well, you have a gentlin' effect on him and that's for shore."

Next, Hank showed her two spring foals gamboling around their mother.

"Twins!" Elizabeth said delightedly.

"Yep," Hank said, looking as though he were personally responsible for it.

Later, walking her back to the house, Hank said, "Shore hope you're planning to stay for the Stampede, Miz Liz. Logan and Red signed up for some of the events, you know."

Elizabeth looked at Hank with interest. "No, I didn't know."

Hank nodded firmly. "Shore. You might say Red challenged Logan, told him he was getting too soft these days." Hank chuckled. "So of course the boss told him he'd enter any event that Red did—and beat him hands down."

"What kind of events, Hank?" Elizabeth knew that the list of events for "The World's Greatest Wild West Show" were endless. There was everything from sharpshooting to steer roping to prize animal stock competitions.

"What do ya think? Bronco bustin' and steer ropin' and the like. Then there's the covered wagon event that's pretty wild. Red signed Logan up for that, too." Hank chuckled hugely this time.

"Sounds like great fun," Elizabeth said a little hesitantly.

"Oh, it'll be that, all right," Hank chortled. "Because I think Logan's gettin' soft, too. On account of all that book writin' he does when he thinks no one's noticing."

"What?" Elizabeth turned to him in surprise.

"Why, shore," Hank said, obviously aware that he had her complete attention. "Elvira's told me plenty of times not to bother the boss 'cause he's doing up one of them textbooks for the agricultural colleges."

"What?" Elizabeth said again, stopping and facing Hank. "Are you sure about this, Hank? Logan hasn't mentioned a thing about it to me."

Hank nodded vigorously. "I'm shore. Yep. Elvira's never one to make things up."

Elizabeth absorbed this carefully, and then proceeded once again. "Now don't be sayin' anything to him about it 'cause like I said...he feels kind of funny about it. The one time I mentioned it, he got mad as thunder—as if he didn't expect anyone to know. I never mentioned it again, 'cause I didn't want to get Elvira into any trouble. Seems to me like he's a little embarrassed about it, you know?"

"Yes...I think I understand, Hank," Elizabeth replied.

"Do you? I shore don't. Hell, if'n I could spell, maybe I'
write me a book, too. And, heck, everyone here knows L
gan made it his business to get a good education. His mam
made sure of that. She was the one to get him going on thos
correspondence courses way back when. Why, I bet by no
he's got one of the P and D's or some such thing."

"That's Ph.D., Hank."

"Huh? Well, what does it mean?"

"If it's true, it means Logan could be a professor at a un
versity."

"What?" Hank pulled at her arm as he broke into wil
mirth. "Now can you jus' see that, Miz Liz? Logan in one
them black dresses those professors wear? What's he gonn
do with his spurs? Use them for slicing up frogs?" Han
wheezed, coughed and gasped for breath.

Elizabeth gave Hank a critical look. "Professors don't ne
essarily wear black gowns, Hank. And the frog-cuttin
business is done in about the eighth or ninth grade. If this
the sort of reaction Logan can expect to get, then it's no wo
der he wants to keep his intellectual goals under wrap
Shame on you, Hank."

"Yes'm," Hank said, trying hard to control himself.

"Besides, Logan would be doing this for his own satisfa
tion only. When a person has a keen mind, he wants to e
ercise it, see what his potential is. Logan would't think
giving up this ranch to go and teach in a city, even if he h
the degrees to do so. But the textbook writing end of it…no
that's a perfect blend, isn't it? Like having his cake and eatin
it, too. And I think that's pretty wonderful."

Hank now looked thoroughly subdued.

"Then, too, if he simply wanted to teach agriculture, h
wouldn't need a degree like that or anything approaching
His qualifications as a cattle rancher alone would be suff
cient. So you see, Hank? Some people play chess, others c
lect degrees—but neither group would think of uprootin

themselves on account of it, or trying to change their basic natures." Elizabeth no longer knew if she were saying all this for Hank's benefit or her own—it seemed she was really just thinking out loud. "Why, Logan is as much a part of all this as..." She gazed around her, looking for an apt comparison, and saw the huge elms that cast their shade over the main house. "As those elms are a part. You can't transplant them because their roots are too deep. But even if you could, they would never thrive as well in any other setting."

"Heck, Miz Liz," Hank said. "I know all that. That's why I broke up like I did. Logan wouldn't want to go and live in any dangblasted city. A man would have to be crazy."

Elizabeth could think of nothing at all to add to that.

Later in her room, as she began to prepare herself for an evening on the town with Logan, she found herself wondering how he would dress. She had yet to see him in anything other than working clothes. Try as she would, she couldn't envision him dressed in a suit. He wore his denims like a second skin. They and the man just naturally went together. She decided he'd probably opt for a casual, Western-style suit and manage to look extremely good in it.

Logan had told her to dress up, but Elizabeth was in a bit of a quandary as to how dressed up to get. After a lot of indecision, she chose a starkly simple, black dinner dress—its pizzazz in the back, which plunged to her waist. On either side, a curve of breast was seen whenever she moved her arms, but from the front the dress was very demure, with a high neckline, a fitted waist, and a soft skirt that flared beautifully when she walked. With a lacy shawl draped around her shoulders for warmth and propriety, she knew she'd feel perfectly at ease walking down any street.

She brushed her hair back in a smooth, soigné style, but then changed her mind and allowed it to fall free, bouncy and full, from crown to shoulders. With diamond earrings in place, and three-inch-high black satin sandals sexily arching her feet, she deemed herself ready for Logan.

8

"YOU'VE BECOME NOTHING BUT A LOVE SLAVE," Elizabeth muttered aloud, helping herself to a drink in Logan's study in order to counteract the mad fluttering of butterflies in her stomach. "And that's a sad state of affairs." Life hadn't taught her anything, she mused. She should be busily haunted by the specter of her mother's vulnerability. She *should* be phoning Charles—he would be bound to bring her back to earth.

And she definitely should not be sneaking through Logan's desk drawers.

But she sat down with some galley proof sheets, anyway, and swiftly read the first four pages before being interrupted by the sound of an outer door closing. Quickly she slipped the pages back in the drawer, picked up her drink and sauntered casually toward the doorway that led out to the front foyer. She leaned against the frame, feeling her insides shake as she watched Logan scrape off several tons of mud from his boots, littering a mat that Elizabeth sincerely hoped was placed there for that purpose.

As he had not had time to change after the storm, his clothes, too, were in bad shape—wrinkled and grimy. He removed his hat and hung it on a hook, and Elizabeth noted that he looked tired and impatient. An unfiltered cigarette seemed as though it was glued to his bottom lip.

She brought the glass to her lips, the ice cubes making a tinkling sound that alerted him. She watched his eyes widen,

and then drift slowly over her in a journey that left no inch
of her unexplored. Then he began to walk slowly toward her.

The warmth of the liquor had calmed the butterflies, but
now the darkened look in his eyes that spoke of his arousal
made her thankful that she had sought the support of the
doorframe.

"Hi." His voice was as whiskey warm as her drink.

"Hi," she murmured back, knowing her own eyes had become dark pools.

He shook his head at her. "No way," he said huskily. "I'm
not laying a hand on you until I get cleaned up."

She reached out and took the cigarette from his mouth and
then placed it between her own lips. She took a small drag
and then held it balanced between the tips of two polished
fingernails. "In that case," she said softly, "I'll just smoke this
while I'm waiting."

He watched every detail as though she were performing a
sensual ceremony then, looking a little pained, he said,
"You're supposed to help me quit, remember? Instead you've
made smoking into an erotic art."

"Just this once," she returned, her voice low. "By the time
I've smoked it, I expect you to be ready to escort me without
bringing your cancer sticks along."

"Getting tough, huh?"

"Whatever it takes," she returned, her voice suggestive.
Then she decided she had better change the subject—Logan
was beginning to look dangerous.

"I wasn't sure what I should wear. Am I too dressed
up?"

He gave this some thought as his eyes drifted over her once
again. She felt breathless by the time they returned to her
face.

"I don't know," he mused. "Turn around and let me see all
of you."

Letting go of the doorframe carefully, she did a slow-motion pirouette, allowing her shawl to slip down to the elbows.

"This is the way I would like you to look all the time," he said, his words serious, devoid of sensual innuendo. "It's the way you should look all the time, because this is your gift. Bringing beauty and delight to the eyes of the world. I feel lucky—and selfish—having you all to myself for now."

For now. It was funny how two tacked-on words could take all the pleasure and warmth out of a beautiful compliment.

"I'll go and get ready," Logan said abruptly, "and try and do you justice. It'll be hard, but I'm going to make a supreme effort."

By the time James arrived, Logan was ready with proffered arm and a decidedly suave manner. Elizabeth could hardly believe it was the same man. He looked a dream in his fawn-colored, perfectly tailored suit with its Continental styling. He seemed amused by her astonished reaction to his appearance, as though he knew what she had been preparing herself for.

He was Logan, yet he wasn't. He was giving her an altogether different view of himself—gentleman, scholar, witty conversationalist—letting her know that as far as he was concerned, it was an easy game to play.

"All right, I think you've rubbed my face in it enough, don't you?" she finally said, just before they were going to drop a nervous James off and proceed through the city on their own.

"Yeah, but I wouldn't have missed it for the world," James said, pulling to a stop at the curb in front of a nondescript building on one of Calgary's main streets. "Wait until I tell Red and the boys that Logan's turned over a new leaf."

"It's none of Red's business," Logan snapped.

"Just kidding, just kidding," James said, pushing his hesitant way out of the car. "You two can cuddle up front now. The old sinner is about to pay his dues."

"Sorry you can't come with us, James," Logan returned, his good humor seemingly restored.

"Sure you are. And I'm the Pope's uncle."

Elizabeth grasped James's hand when Logan had helped her alight from the back seat, which they had opted to share.

"James, are you really that nervous?" Elizabeth asked sympathetically.

"Yes. But I look on it this way. I've already beaten this thing, so this is just a penance. The worse it is, the better I'll feel."

"But you do plan on continuing with it? Just in case..."

"The will grows weak?" James supplied. "Don't worry, honey. I'd walk on hot coals to make sure I don't slip into my bad ways. You can trust me, Elizabeth," he added, looking into her eyes in an intense way. "So you don't have to be afraid for your mother's sake anymore. Or for your own." He turned and made his way toward the basement steps of the building.

Elizabeth spoke past the lump in her throat. "I really believe him, Logan. You were right—James is all but there. But I have a feeling he's still going to be in for a few home truths tonight, don't you?"

Logan nodded. "I think you're right. But it isn't too soon to say all's well that ends well where James and your mother are concerned. They've paid their dues and they both deserve the good things that are coming."

"Mother said that you had offered to hold the wedding here. Is that true, Logan?"

Logan reached over and grabbed her hand. "That was the original offer, yes, and I don't see any reason to change it now. Just a small ceremony with you and me as witnesses, okay? The big stuff is out of my league."

"I'm beginning to think that nothing is out of your league," Elizabeth murmured, more to herself than to him.

"I beg your pardon, *ma chérie*?"

"Enough, Logan—as I said before, you've proved your point."

"Who said clothes didn't make the man?" he scoffed.

"Where are you taking me?" Driving into the city by night, with its skyline lit up and outlined against the horizon, Elizabeth couldn't help but feel a bit of excitement. Cities at night always did this to her, whereas daylight country vistas usually made her nostalgic. She eagerly took in the sights as they drove along the main drag of the city.

"In this soaring city of oil-fueled progress?" Logan returned. "Gee, I don't know, It's white collar now, Liz'beth...but in a couple of weeks you'll be knee-deep in drugstore cowboys."

"Come on, Logan," she said, laughing.

"The Calgary Stampede, naive one," he said. "The bow-legged struttin' that goes on you wouldn't believe. Dancin' in the streets, by jingles, and Indian war whoops you can hear a mile away."

"I love it. Hank said you and Red had entered some competitions. Can I root for the victor come Stampede time?"

"Depends on who you're going to holler for," Logan said, suddenly looking stern.

"Old stony face himself," she told him. "You, of course. I'd be rooting for you."

"In that case," he said politely, "You can come."

She hit her palm against his biceps. "Listen to the macho hombre beneath those well-tailored duds. And I'll just bet you can really strut when you're hitting your stride. You'd put John Travolta to shame."

"Who?"

"The world will close in on you one of these days, Logan. And then what will you do? *Holler* for mercy?"

"Beats closing your eyes to it," Logan said, his smile twisted.

"You love it, don't you? All...all that you are, I mean. This fancy suit business—it's just for my benefit, isn't it?"

It took him a long while to reply. When he did, it was to say quietly. "I could fit into your world, if I had to."

She felt her heart skip at least two beats. "Perhaps you could, but I doubt if you'd like it," she commented lightly. "Have you ever driven down the main drag of Toronto on a Friday night?"

He shook his head while a smile played about his lips.

"Well, you'd really be in for a treat. All the animals come out to play and it's sheer chaos.

"If it's so terrible, why are you smiling?"

She shrugged and laughed a little. "Because it's fun, I guess. There's a definite hum and throb to it all. The city's alive—you can feel it. Besides, there's something there I'll guarantee you won't find here."

"And what might that be?"

"Giant pretzels with mustard. Soft, hot ones. Every time I see a vendor I make a beeline. Have you ever had one, Logan? Have you ever just smelled one?"

"No, but you sound like a kid in a candy store," he mused, pulling into a parking lot beside a discreetly lettered restaurant and club. "Sounds like your kind of town."

"I guess I do love it at that. What's this place, Logan?"

"It's your everyday intimate little supper club. Good food and a little shuffling on the floor between courses. Not too fancy, but highly respectable."

"Sounds like you know your way around, partner."

"I mosey through town now and again."

"On the prowl?" she asked, tongue in cheek as he turned off the ignition and faced her.

"Stop talking and start kissing," he said, his mouth an inch from hers. "This is going to have to do me for a couple of hours, at least."

Toying with him, she said, "But you haven't answered my question yet." Her finger came up to stroke softly at the lobe of his ear.

"Yes. And I have even made love to one or two or three females. Satisfied?"

Her hand fell down to stroke his biceps, along the fine material of his suit. "That's why you joined up for those events in the Stampede, isn't it? So all the town women will fawn over you when you win everything hands down."

His mouth, so close to hers, quirked. "You don't expect much, do you? I'm getting old, Liz'beth, and there are days when the bones I've broken on the hard, dusty ground poke a friendly reminder at me. Red railroaded me into this, and now I've got to go through with it or I won't be able to live it down. Many moons ago I won my share of prizes, so I'm just as content to let the younger guys compete for the spoils. Red, you may have noticed, is a younger guy."

"Then you think he's going to beat you?"

"He will in the Brahma-bull event."

Elizabeth felt the roots of her hair prickle. "What? You don't mean to tell me you are actually going to ride one of those things?"

"Have to," he said, simply. "Red signed me up."

"Well, unsign yourself!"

"Are we going to kiss here or what?"

"*Or what.* Logan, promise me you won't do anything so stupid. I thought it would just be steer roping and...Oh, you know...sharpshooting and stuff."

"Well, this is the 'stuff' part," he said, giving her nose a soft stroke. "And don't worry—I'm still pretty good at stuff."

She continued the argument during and after the kissing, and then brought it up again during their dinner. "A Brahma bull, for God's sake!"

Patiently, Logan said, "It's just another form of bronco riding."

"Bull."

"That's the form."

"Logan, I don't consider this a joking matter. What if you fall off?"

Logan, in the process of taking a drink from his glass of water, almost choked. Dabbing at his mouth with a napkin, he said, "Now *you're* joking. Honey, I expect to fall off. One just hopes for later rather than sooner. Besides, there are other events that are a lot worse than the bull riding."

"Name them," Elizabeth said with a flinty-eyed look. "And then tell me that you aren't signed up for them."

"Actually I think we ought to change the subject."

Elizabeth laid down her fork. "I won't eat another thing until you tell me."

"Good, because I've never seen such a healthy appetite," he said, referring to the one small crab leg and the sliver of steak remaining on her plate.

She continued to glare at him.

"I'll tell you later."

"When?"

"In bed tonight."

His quietly uttered statement abruptly put a halt to her glaring look. She cast her lashes down, unable to make contact with his eyes for the moment. Finally she lifted them and said, "I haven't phoned Charles yet."

"So?" Logan said, covering his reaction to her words.

"So I think I should, don't you?"

Logan tossed down his napkin and reached in his breast pocket for his cigarettes, then frowned when he realized they weren't there. Keeping the frown, he said, "Let's get out of here, okay? I'll tread on your feet another time."

Not liking his change of mood, she merely nodded, feeling a sense of regret that they had not danced. She knew that Logan would do that well, too.

He placed the shawl around her shoulders when she rose from her chair, and then escorted her from the dimly lit atmosphere with a light hand on the small of her back. In the lobby, Elizabeth said nothing as he worked the cigarette machine, noting only that he chose a filtered brand this time.

Outside, as he lit up, he said, "Don't say it."

"I wouldn't dare," she replied.

"Do you want to walk for a while? James still has a half an hour to go," he said, looking at his watch.

"What I really wanted to do was dance."

He placed his arm around her waist. "Our dance six years ago wasn't enough for you? Me and my flat feet?"

She saw that he was attempting to snap out of his mood and knew it would be best if she didn't mention Charles again. Really it was up to her what she did in that quarter, and of course it would be a touchy subject, under the circumstances. She tried to imagine how she would feel if Logan had brought up one of his girlfriends' names in connection with the two of them sleeping together, and she suddenly could not blame him in the least for his bad mood. She would not make such a stupid mistake again.

"You dance like you do everything else, Logan. I can remember clearly being swept off my feet in a grand manner."

"That's a good girl. Soothe the ruffled beast. As it is, he can't wait to sweep you off your feet in another way."

"I've been wined and dined and...warned, have I?"

He stopped her in the middle of the walkway, in front of a darkened drugstore window. "Lady, I love you," he murmured, bringing his mouth to hers in a brief, but intensely stirring kiss. "And tonight I want to show you how much. You may have noticed that I can't stop touching you, but, sweetheart, this is only the beginning...."

Logan stayed at the wheel for the long drive home, while James sat in the back regaling them with a minute-by-minute account of the meeting he had just attended. He told them about a bank manager who had been brought up on charges owing to his misappropriation of funds. The money was to feed the gambling, of course, which had already put him hopelessly into debt.

"This guy was a highly respected citizen, you know?" James went on. "Both he and his wife are churchgoers and well-known and highly regarded in the community. The newspapers had a field day when he was caught. His wife left him and took their two kids shortly after some bank customers began to dump their garbage on his front lawn. He's still awaiting sentencing, but his lawyer told him the judge would take his attendance at these meetings as a first step in trying to rehabilitate himself. He'll probably get a suspended sentence. Then there's this other guy..."

As James talked, carefully avoiding names, Elizabeth closed here eyes and smiled to herself. She felt light and airy and happy, for both James's sake and her own.

"So after this new guy got up there and told his story, I thought—why not? Compared to the stories of some of these men, and women, too, mine was pretty mundane. So I just said simply that the only thing standing between me and the woman I loved was the gambling that still could get out of control, despite the fact that I thought I'd licked it." James reached into his pocket and withdrew a sheet of paper. "But I've got help anytime I need it, right here. A name and a phone number I can call any time of the day or night. I'm supposed to write it down alongside the numbers of the police and the fire department. His name is Dan, and he's a hell of a guy. We spent a lot of time talking about why I maybe took it up and let it get out of control like I did. A lot of what he said made sense," James finished thoughtfully.

"This guy has put it all behind him?" Logan inquired.

"Yeah, he sure has. Had to lose everything before he smartened up, though. That's why he says he wants to help, if he can. He says he likes to latch on to the fellows who haven't lost everything—yet."

A silence ensued after that, James obviously falling deep into thought. Elizabeth rubbed her arms beneath her shawl and Logan shifted a little in his seat. Finally Logan said, "I think maybe you've just had a narrow escape, my friend."

"Yeah. Something just skipped lightly over my grave, all right."

No more was said after that.

When they arrived at the Opal L, James took his place behind the wheel and regarded them both. "I take it there's no sense in my asking what's going on between the two of you?"

"In that case," Logan said, "you'll understand why I'm not asking you in for a drink."

James frowned a little. "That's my daughter you've got hold of there, you know. It seems to me I ought to say something."

Elizabeth smiled at James. "Why don't you telephone tomorrow. By then you'll probably have thought of something."

"If it were anyone else but Logan..." he muttered. He frowned, put the car in gear and drove away.

"Once a father, always a father," Logan said, leaning down to kiss her cheek.

"You're lucky he likes you so much," she replied as they walked up the steps.

"Oh, I'm lucky all right," Logan agreed, looking at her with a passionate light in his eyes.

The moment they entered the house, Elvira, dressed in a cotton robe, came forward to say, "A man has been phoning for you, Miss Jackson. He asks that you phone him back. I have his name written here," she finished, pulling a slip of paper from her pocket. "He says you have his number."

Elizabeth needed only a glance at the name. "Yes. Thank you, Elvira."

Elvira walked off while Elizabeth darted a quick look up at Logan.

"Well? What are you waiting for?" he said. "You wanted to ask his permission, didn't you?"

Elizabeth looked away from his hard features. "No. I don't feel that way anymore. But..."

"But what?"

"Charles loves me, Logan. He deserves to know what I'm up to."

He looked down at her for a long, silent moment. Finally he said, "Aren't you a little afraid of burning all your bridges? If you tell him, he might take a walk."

Elizabeth slowly looked up at him, her heart sinking as she did. "He might," she agreed, trying to keep her voice composed.

"Wouldn't you care?"

"I was quite willing to take the chance," she said, her voice fairly cool now.

"In spite of the fact that you were all set to move in with him?"

She closed her eyes briefly. "I wasn't set to move in with him. I lied to you about that."

"Why?"

Becoming impatient, she said, "What is this, Logan? Twenty questions? I had my reasons, okay?"

He grasped her wrist as he grated harshly, "Dammit—what do you think I'm made of? I want some answers, Elizabeth. You put me through hell and then you calmly tell me that you lied? I need to know exactly how things stand between you and Durney."

She tried to twist out of his grasp. "You're hurting me, Logan! How can I tell you anything when you're behaving like a Neanderthal?"

"A Neanderthal," he repeated, nodding his head slowly. "I suppose that's how I must seem to you half the time." Suddenly he was dragging her into the study, heedless of the fact that she nearly tripped and that her shawl had fallen to the floor. Once they were in the dimly lighted sanctuary of the room, he took her into a crushing embrace and subjected her to hard, hungry kisses. Gasping when he released her, she brought her fingers to her bruised mouth as he said softly, "That, my dear Liz, is a *Neanderthalism*. That is what I refrain from doing every time you mention Durney's name. What does he do when he gets angry? Lift your hand and smack his lips against it in a no-nonsense manner?"

Her eyes brimming, she said, "You don't know what you're talking about, Logan. If...if you knew Cha—if you knew him, you would probably like him. You're overreacting. Besides, you said you were entirely unconcerned about him."

"Elizabeth," he said, dragging his hand through his hair as he looked at her tears, "Try to understand me. A few hours ago I told you that I loved you. Did you think those were casual words? Now...now you're telling me that another man loves you. So the question here is, how do you feel, sweetheart? I'm in the dark and you won't answer one simple question I put to you. Don't you love me back a little, Liz?"

She could hardly believe that he even needed to ask the question. She thought she had given herself away in a hundred different ways. She loved all things about him—every nuance of expression, every subtle voice change. She could not even feel roused to anger over his roughness toward her; the compensation had been feeling his hard warm body and the intensity of the hunger in his lips. She could fall at his feet, she loved him so much. And it was this knowledge alone that seemed to force her to speak out angrily.

"One simple question, Logan? You've never stopped badgering me about Charles! But all right. I'll tell you why I lied to you! Does self-protection cover it? I'd have to be a fool to want to put myself through all this, wouldn't I?" The tears she had tried to keep at bay once again welled up in her eyes.

"You say you love me. I wonder if you really know what love—true, unselfish love—is. Men like Charles do. Yes, it's true, so don't bother to try and cut off my circulation again because even so—even so—you've won, Logan! You may want to know that I have never even slept with Charles!" Her tears fell freely now. "I do love you. But I wish I didn't! By the time this is over, there isn't going to be enough of me left. I hate this kind of love. I never wanted it," she continued on a ragged breath. "It took me years to get over you the first time—if I ever really did—and now you've put me back at square one," she accused through her tears. "How could you do that to me, Logan? How could you do that if you really loved me?"

"Liz'beth. . .shh," he said, hauling her close, his arms around her in soothing comfort.

Her tears streaked his jacket as she pressed her face against his chest. "You practically broke my wrist," she further accused.

He kissed the top of her head. "Sweetheart, I'd cut my heart out rather than hurt you."

"That's what James said about Mother. Look at all the hurt she's had to bear."

He understood the deeper meaning of her words. "I'm not James, and you're not your mother. You can't live for and through a man; no one expects you to. You talk about unselfish love, Liz'beth—don't you know by now that I've been trying my damnedest? But I'm only human, sweetheart. This time around I needed my stardust, I needed to know that you still loved me a little."

"More than a little. Do you think. . .isn't there any way the twain can meet for us? I keep thinking about when the time comes to—"

"Shh, I know. Don't dwell on it. Liz'beth, we still have some time ahead of us."

She felt as though a vise were squeezing her heart. "Is that going to be enough for you?" she questioned, her face still against his chest. His heartbeat was so steady, so rhythmic.

"It will have to be, won't it?"

She swallowed hard. "Well, what's so terrible, so frightening—" she tried to laugh a little "—is that if you asked it of me I probably would give up—"

The slight movement of his body told her that he was already shaking his head.

"And live to regret it," he said. His voice sounded heavy. "They say the world is well lost for love, but personally I've always found that a pretty fanciful notion. Sooner or later, awareness of the world and self-knowledge creep in. I firmly believe that, Liz'beth. That's why whoever's doing the sacrificing has to be damn sure they're doing the right thing. For the sake of both." He sighed heavily. "This isn't making either of us feel better, but I guess we had to get into it eventually. I'd only hoped to put off the inevitable for a while longer."

"I do love the ranch, Logan," she said, lifting her face to wipe her eyes.

"I know you do," he returned. "But we're talking about an entirely different life-style. You'd never make it, honey. And I'd never see that beautiful face of yours adorning magazine covers. I sneak a look at Elvira's collection from time to time."

Her smile was weak. "And you are this ranch, Logan. In my mind I see you as inseparable from it. If there was any sacrificing to be done it would have to be me."

"You can't see me jogging in Toronto in my spurs?"

"Don't tease. I couldn't laugh now if I tried. I know you're an educated man, Logan. Hank spilled the beans, and I've already peeked at one of your textbook manuscripts. So, as you said, you could fit into another life-style if you *had* to. But that's the operative word, isn't it? It doesn't allow for choice and free will or what you really want in life, so I would never ask that of you." She sighed tremulously. "That leaves

us at square one again. Then, too, you haven't said a word
about marriage or permanence; you've been very careful not
to. So this conversation is really irrelevant, isn't it?" She
waited a second or two and then rushed on. "What we really
have here is a summer romance, one in which there are no
strings attached. Therefore, you have no right to question me
about Charles or any other man."

"That's quite a wrap-up."

"Do you have anything to add?" Her face was muffled
against his chest once again, and she could hear the solid
beating of his heart ticking off the time it took him to respond.

"What can I add at this point? You've sprung this on me a
little too soon, Liz'beth. I had hoped to—"

"Sleep with me several times first?" she broke in, stepping
away from his warmth.

He shook his head at her. "Don't do this, Elizabeth. I can't
help wanting you. Would my asking you to marry me this
minute solve the problem?"

She stared at him a moment, and then suddenly waves of
self-disgust coursed through her. "God," she moaned. "What
am I doing to you, Logan? What am I doing to myself?" She
looked at him pityingly. "Six years have gone by, haven't
they? Or did I just dream dignity and self-assurance and independence? Logan, you poor man. I apologize profusely for
trying to force a marriage proposal out of you...one that
common sense dictates I'd have to turn down. That's saying
if I could hunt some up, of course. I don't seem to have the
ability to be coolheaded and clear thinking the way you are."

"Elizabeth," he said, attempting to stop her from berating
herself, but she swiftly shook her head.

"I mean...after all...it's only been a few days and nights
since I got here, and ten hours or so since you made love to
me...you might well say I've sprung this on you a little too
soon." She looked down at the floor and then over at his feet

"Where is my pride? I know I dropped it around here some-where."

Logan made a move toward her, but she backed off, once again shaking her head. "No, Logan, you have no idea the kind of fool I can make out of myself if you touch me." She folded her hands and brought her knuckles to her chin. "Who gave you this power? Could you please tell them—devil or gods—to take it back? It isn't fair!"

"Elizabeth, stop this!" he said harshly. "You're getting hysterical."

"So would you be if you'd just lost part of your identity!"

"I'm fixing you a drink," he said, walking swiftly over to the bar.

"You don't need to! You can seduce me easily without it."

"A double," he muttered, and after a second's thought, poured the same amount of whiskey for himself.

He handed it to her carefully, making sure he kept his distance from the angry wariness in her eyes. She had never looked more beautiful to him or more desirable, and he could feel his body aching with the knowledge. He knew he could come up with the right words—the words that would bring her into his arms. He also knew he couldn't do that unless he were one hundred percent sure that he could back them up. He felt frustrated and saddened by the shambles the evening had become, his mind and body wanting her so much he knew he hardly dared to look at her.

After he had watched her take one hesitant sip of her drink and then another, he followed suit. "This is just as hard for me, Liz'beth. I want you to know that. If I seem clearheaded to you, it's only because I've had six years to think this through and try to come up with some sort of answer. You might think yourself willing to be the sacrificial lamb, but I know better. In a year—maybe two—from now, you'll hate me and all that I stand for. You're a tropical bird, Elizabeth, and keeping you out here would be like caging you in a henhouse. Maybe you don't know that yet. Maybe you haven't become acquainted well enough with your basic nature. You're still pretty young, so I think perhaps you're just going to have to trust me on that."

He took a heavy swallow of his drink, and then moved farther away from her—out of the range of the seductive scent she wore. "You try hard to fit in here, Liz'beth, offering your services to all and sundry. Yes," he affirmed, catching her look, "I heard the latest from Hank. But if you think I'm going to let you cook for my men, you've got another think coming."

"I'm simply to be your dress-up doll for the summer, is that it?" she demanded angrily. "Is that all the form and substance I have in your opinion? I mean, what does a tropical bird do all day, Logan? Apart from sitting in a tree preening its feathers?"

"If you're going to scoff at tropical birds, Elizabeth, then you might as well scoff at sunsets and flowers and rainbows and the *Mona Lisa*. The world would be a drab and mundane place without them. And I'm not a shallow man, Liz'beth. When I fall in love it's with a flesh-and-blood woman, not a dream image. So don't talk to me about dress-up dolls and a lack of substance. To me, you're as precious on the inside as you are on the outside—and I'd love you wart, granny-glasses, and all."

She looked at him helplessly.

"Then there's the other side of the coin," he said, taking a deep breath. "I look at you and I think, 'I would go to the end of the earth for this woman.'" His eyes were burning ember as he looked at her. "'She's Liz'beth—and I've loved her with a passion since she was sixteen years old.' God save me! When you left, the world turned gray for me." He shook his head sadly. "All the rainbows went away with you."

"Oh, Logan," she whispered softly, taking a hesitant step toward him.

"No. Stay there, Liz'beth. There's more. I have to tell you all of it," he said, pain etching his features. "I sent you away because I knew you didn't belong here. For a long time afterward, I had to stop myself from wanting to go after you and bring you back. It got so that I couldn't concentrate on anything else. All I knew was that I wanted you and it was a physical ache inside me. So—" he exhaled heavily "—I thought if I was going to crash into your world one of these days then I'd better prepare myself for it. I'd better have more than sweat and prime beef stock to offer you, because I knew that once the world caught sight of you, I'd be lucky just to shoulder my way in."

He took a swallow of his drink and looked at her. "So I decided to do a make-over job on myself, give myself a few alternative paths I could take in this world. And I guess you've discovered some of them, Elizabeth. I *could* play the sophisticate. I *could* teach in some agricultural college or maybe even a higher institute of learning. I *could* live in the city— any city—or just live the author's life and enjoy a slower pace. Financially cushioned by the sale of this ranch," he finished quietly.

The words hung in the air between them for several seconds.

"By the sale of my life."

Tears welled up in her eyes as she looked at him, and she was suddenly recalling an image she had formed upon first catching sight of him at the airport. He had looked then as he looked now. A man coming face-to-face with himself after intense soul-searching.

She shook her head at him. "Never," she breathed. "Never, Logan. I'd never let you."

"I knew you'd say that. But don't think it makes me feel one iota better. I am what I am, Elizabeth. I think I need this ranch like an addict needs his fix. Whenever I'm away from it I feel as though I've left a large chunk of myself behind. I could give

it up for you—no one else but you, Liz'beth—but I'm afrai
of the regrets that might eat us up later."

"Logan," Elizabeth said softly, her throat aching wit
unshed tears as she looked at him helplessly.

He shook his head. "We're both having the same proble
here. If I take you in my arms now, which I *badly* want to do
I'll never be able to let you go. I'm going to stop kidding my
self about that, too. And if we got married—"

Elizabeth felt her breath catch.

"—there couldn't ever be a divorce, you see. I don't be
lieve in divorce. No matter how unhappy you got living ou
here, I couldn't let you go." He sighed. "So, no." He shook hi
head firmly. "A sacrifice from you is only going to mean gu
wrenching pain for me down the road."

Elizabeth's heart felt full to bursting. The knowledge tha
Logan loved her—had always loved her with a torment suc
as this—was eclipsing the bitter facts of the situation. Sh
recognized his wisdom and knew she ought to bow to it, kne
that the years he had on her gave him the insight to see be
yond this heart-wrenching, mind-dissolving moment in the
lives. She knew it, but all she wanted of time and of fate an
of the world was for Logan to take her into his arms and mak
love to her with the fury and strength of their combined pas
sion.

Her thickly lashed eyes moved over him hungrily, watche
him staring down into his drink with his face set and his ja
clenched. In her mind's eye, she was already kissing the frow
lines away, slipping his beautiful suit jacket off his shoul
ders, undoing his tie, unbuttoning his sensual silk shir
parting the edges to view the brawn beneath, touching he
tongue to the hard flesh...

She could feel her nipples hardening with demand. "Lo
gan," she said huskily, hearing the raw need in her own voice
"Has Elvira gone to bed, do you think?"

His eyes met hers across the room in a puzzled, questioning look. "Probably. But that's a hell of a change in subject, Liz'beth."

"Would you just close and lock the door for a moment, Logan? There's something I have to show you."

She thought it amazing, but there was no awareness on his face as he regarded her. "What is it?"

"Just something I think you should know about."

There was only one table lamp burning, its soft light just catching her in its glow. As Logan obligingly walked to the door, Elizabeth slipped off her black lace panties and tucked the wisp of material between the pages of a book on Logan's desk. She had picked the book at random and didn't glance at the title until she was holding it in both hands. A smile touched her lips.

"Should I draw the curtains and bolt the windows, too?" he asked, with a slight curve of his lips. "What's so secretive?"

She glanced at the windows and saw that the curtains were already drawn. Elizabeth shook her head. "It's just something in regard to this book of yours," she said, handing it over to him.

He took it with a wry grimace. "*Lady Chatterley's Lover,*" he murmured. "Kate's little joke on my birthday. Said it would likely round out my education."

Kate was a subject for another time and another place. "Well...I've marked a spot, Logan. I really think you ought to take a look at it," Elizabeth said, raising her arms to the back of her neck to work at the fastening of her dress.

Logan's head was bent to the book, which quite naturally fell open to Elizabeth's marker. As he picked up the lacy garment between thumb and forefinger, the bodice of Elizabeth's dress dropped down to hang from the fitted waist.

When he looked up at her, alert sensuality in his gaze, her hands were at her sides, her chin raised to meet his look.

He stared at her, speechless, for long moments, his eyes drinking in the seductive beauty she had presented him with. Carelessly the book slipped from his fingers and thudded to the floor.

Elizabeth moistened her lips. "If this is all we're going to get, Logan," she said huskily, "don't you think we ought to make the very best of it? I suggest we start here...in this terribly studious room."

But he had not finished reveling in the sight of her yet: her glistening lips, the full roundness of rosy-tipped breasts, the sheen of her flaming hair. At last, as though he were making an effort to step out of a dream, he looked down at the bit of lace he still held, feeling the reality of its texture.

"Perhaps you'll just slip those in your pocket for me," Elizabeth ventured, feeling the waiting vibrancy in the room. The very air seemed electric, raising the fine hairs on her arms.

He did as she suggested. Then he was reaching for her, and she toppled toward him, as if drawn by a magnet. "Logan," she breathed against his neck, feeling the immediate crushing strength of his embrace. "Oh, how I love the way you look at me. Tell me you understand and feel the same way. That you don't think badly of me for this."

He told her with his lips and his hands and his body before he even uttered a word. With his mouth hot against hers, his hands cupping and stroking her, his desire pressing thick and hard against her, he growled, "Think badly of you? Are you out of your mind, woman? You intoxicate me. I'm drunk on your beauty and your sexiness. Liz'beth, you angel, you can do all this any time of the day or night. I'll give you a whistle, and if I happen to be out on the range, or..."

A deep, voracious, drowning kiss replaced his words, and Elizabeth knew how it felt to be devoured by passion. He seemed not to know which part of her to kiss and taste next. She clung to him, reeling under his dynamite assault, her own plans for his body swept aside by the needs of his hands and lips.

"Liz'beth, I'm not feeling in the least studious. All I can think about is having you upstairs in my bed."

"Oh, yes," she breathed, "Only it had better be soon, or you'll have to carry me."

With that, he immediately lifted her into his arms, cradling her high, as if she weighed nothing at all. "I think I can manage that," he said, his eyes locked with hers.

"There's an awful lot of stairs," she reminded him, though reveling in his strength.

"Did you take out your contacts?" he asked.

"Yes. Why?"

"Your eyes are so dark that they look purple."

"The color of passion, they say."

"I love you, Elizabeth. More now than ever before."

With that, she melted. She placed her mouth to the ridge of his jaw, traced her tongue along it, then said with whispery softness, "Anything, Logan. Anything you want to do…it's what I want, too. I love you so much that I ache with it."

His reaction to those statements would have left her breathless, she knew, but in the throbbing silence that preceded his response, an unexpected sound came to them, drawing them both up in the same instant. It was a creaking sound—the sound of a cautious footstep walking on a loose floorboard. Both turned their heads, Logan with a soft oath, as they looked at the window that faced the porch. Then he was looking down at Elizabeth. As though stricken, she was staring at the slight gap in the drapes. A parting so small it had previously escaped all attention.

"Let me down, Logan," she said, pushing at his chest in distress.

"Easy, honey," he soothed, putting her down, but his features spoke a different story, his brow beginning to furrow with anger.

"Oh, Logan," Elizabeth said, fumbling with the top of her dress. "How long do you suppose...? Who would do a thing like that?"

Logan had begun to push her ahead of him toward the door. "I don't know," he said, "but I'm going to find out. You go on upstairs and wait for me. I'll be damned if I'll have a Peeping Tom employed on my ranch."

She waited for him in his room, pacing back and forth, wondering what Logan would do to the intruder when he caught him. His face had looked like a thundercloud as he had swiftly exited the house. She was wishing now that she had not reacted with such mortification, for she knew that had added greatly to the eruption of Logan's anger. Whoever the Peeping Tom was, he had not seen all that much of her, she kept telling herself. Logan's back had faced the window much of the time. Her flesh prickled and crawled. She closed her eyes and blessed the fact that she had not been quite bold enough to remove her dress completely.

Red, she though suddenly, and for no justifiable reason she could think of. His name was just suddenly there, and then his face, with a certain look in the eyes that gave credence to the flash thought. On the trail of that came the vision of a violent fight between two men, one younger than the other— Logan slowly but surely losing ground. By the time she heard him calling to her from the direction of her bedroom, she was frantic.

"I'm in here," she quickly replied, grateful that he sounded so healthy and whole. She moved into his arms the moment he came through the door, his face having told her he hadn't caught whoever it was.

"If I ever find out who it was, I'll kill the bastard," he swore, pulling her close against him.

"I don't want to talk about it," she whispered. "Just hold me."

"You're shivering," he observed, a tightness in his voice.

"I was worried that you'd get into a fight and come out the loser."

"Impossible. I'm the good guy, remember?" He was obviously attempting to lighten his tone for her sake. "Sweetheart, are you going to be all right?"

"Yes, Logan. I am all right. I'm more upset over how upset you are than anything else. And I'm shivering because I feel cold. Let's turn out the lights and get under the covers. But first promise me you won't kill anybody on my account. Whoever it was really saw next to nothing. It could even have been someone looking to see if you were still up. Maybe there was a problem with the stock or something. That's possible, isn't it?"

"Yes, Liz'beth, it's possible," he said. By the slowness of his reply she realized that he was thinking of the one man who would be most likely to relay such a message. She acted quickly, before Logan could voice his thoughts. Reaching past him, she flicked off the light, saying, "Let's not talk about it now. Do you or do you not want to go to bed with me?"

"You know I do, but I have a feeling you aren't really in the mood. You're just trying to divert my killer instincts." He nuzzled her neck warmly just the same.

"I want you beside me, Logan—in the dark, holding me, talking softly. Do you have any idea what the sound of your voice does to me?"

"I think I'm diverted," he growled seductively.

They undressed quickly, and in moments they were lying together, the length of their bodies touching under the thick, protective covers.

"You feel so good," Logan groaned, then his mouth was warm on hers.

And so do you, she thought. Lying close to him like this was so luxurious that she wanted to revel in it all night. But she found herself unable to relax. Whenever she closed her eyes, she would see Red's face, his eyes looking her over as they had earlier that day. She must have shuddered a little, for Logan immediately broke the kiss.

The moonlight illuminated her face as she looked up at him, and he could see that her eyes were moist.

"I feel cheated," she told him. "And it makes me damn mad."

"I think I know what you mean, but tell me, anyway."

She rolled her head on the pillow before speaking. "It was magic—pleasure, excitement, loving you so much, knowing how you felt about me. Wanting it to be perfect. Oh, damn. You know what I mean!"

"I'm afraid I do," he replied. "But you wanted me to control my killer instincts, remember?"

"Oh, Logan. I guess we have to talk about it, after all. You suspect Red, too, don't you?"

Logan lay back on his pillow, and the sound he made brought forth the image of a lion with a thorn in its paw. It took him a while to respond. "He has that kind of interest in you, Liz'beth. I've always known that. But by rights he would have been out on the range for the night." After a moment, Logan continued his speculation. "Of course the herd is close enough that he could have easily ridden here after dark in the hope that he might catch you alone." He swore softly. "I'll bet his mind has been on you all day."

"You can't be sure about any of this, Logan."

"That's what's so damn frustrating about it. I can't fire a man on the basis of suspicions. Especially a man I value as much as I do Red. He can run this place as well as I can, Liz'beth, and he knows it. There's always been this tendency on his part to compete with me, which may be where you come into it."

"You said Kate loves him. How does he feel about her?"

"He's generally pretty attentive toward her. I think he likes and respects her. But he's been dragging his feet for years now, so I doubt if he's ever going to pop the question. If he did, it would solve a lot of our problems," he finished, turning toward her.

"What do you mean?" she asked softly.

"I mean...apart from the way he makes me grit my teeth whenever he looks at you, I like Red. He's trustworthy and reliable in all matters concerning the ranch, for one thing. But he isn't family and, as I said, there's this element of competition between us. Kate, on the other hand, would always have my best interests at heart. Between the two of them, the ranch would always be here waiting for us, wouldn't it? And in the meantime, any other place in the world could be our playground for as many years as we wanted it to be. As long as we could come back here every summer...I would need to do that."

No other words were possible for him, for Elizabeth was kissing him wildly and hugging him with all her strength.

"Logan," she breathed finally, pressing tightly against him, "What an absolutely perfect solution! I would always want to come back here, too!"

He brought his hands up to her hair and looked into her eyes. "Shh, love...it's only wishful thinking. Red hasn't proposed to Kate, and he may well be our Peeping Tom. Until I know one way or the other, do you think I'd want him marrying my half sister?"

Elizabeth came down to earth with a heavy thud. Only Logan's arms cushioned her fall. "For a minute there, I was in heaven," she said sadly.

"Which proves what I've been saying all along. You don't want to give up your world completely, any more than I want to give up mine. Tell me, Liz'beth. Tell me all the things you love about your life. Maybe that way I can keep my mind off...other things," he finished, his voice strained.

He loosened his hold on her, and she lay back against her pillow, realizing the embrace she had subjected him to had all but destroyed his control. But she wanted the timing to be just right and, obviously, so did he. She willed her body to relax and let her thoughts drift. With a slight smile, she began to speak softly, "Well, I guess there are lots of things I love. I love working for a living; I like the feeling of worth and pride it gives me. That's what came of you calling me spoiled and pampered princess. Remember, Logan?"

"A little too well. My delicate way of handling that situation left something to be desired."

"Well, that's all in the past. Where was I? Oh yes, there's my dance classes and my acting lessons. I have several favorite eating spots where I love to go—you know my appetite. And there's this old dive that still manages to book the cream of the jazz musicians, so I guess it has its own rough kind of charm. I hang out there with my acting class sometimes."

"I didn't know you were thinking of becoming an actress."

"Doesn't every model? The commercials have given me good visibility, and now it seems all I need to do is learn how to act. I've already received offers, but I don't want to be cast just for my looks."

Logan exhaled. "And you were actually thinking of giving all that up to be chief cook and bottle washer on this ranch? Are you out of your mind, Liz'beth?"

"Put like that..."

"Damn right. You had brain fever there for a while, but I'm going to take your temperature fairly often from here on in. Go on, sweetheart, tell me more. If we do manage to work things out between us, I want to know all there is to know about your life. What about people, friends?"

"I've been too busy working to really cultivate friendships. I think my mother is possibly my best friend. And then there's Luke." She slanted a look at Logan. "Yes, I'd definitely have to say I love Luke, even though he can be incredibly demanding."

"You'd better explain this relationship," Logan said, apparently withholding judgment.

She smiled. "Luke is my photographer. We've practically lived together over the past few months. But don't worry, Logan, he's gay."

"I'm glad to hear that. Okay, Luke's well accounted for. Who else?"

"Just...Charles...but you already know about him," she said with some hesitation, then rushed on, "And my grandparents, of course. Grandmother is something of a dragon, as you've no doubt heard, but I love and respect her all the same. And Grandpa is a real sweetie. They'd be terribly lonely if both Mother and I moved so far away."

"This is the lady you think might invite me into her drawing room?" Logan inquired dryly.

"Well...she did have her heart set on Charles. But usually anything I do is all right with her. She thinks I'm so levelheaded and wise that she can't conceive of me making any sort of mistake. Therefore, she'd look upon you as 'Elizabeth's chosen' and an 'interesting new find'?"

"I see. Saint Elizabeth, hmm?"

"Well...not quite." With that, Elizabeth turned on her side and moved splayed fingers over his chest, feeling its texture, the steady rise and fall.

"Liz'beth," he half groaned, "What are you trying to do to me?"

"I'm just reveling."

"Is that what you call it?"

"Mmm."

"Would it be all right if I reveled a little, too?"

"I think you should..."

He did not reply with words; instead, he sought out h
mouth with hunger no longer contained.

9

A LONG TIME LATER, Logan said, "You know what this means, don't you?"

"For richer or poorer, in sickness or in health. On this ranch, in Toronto, or on the moon..."

"Wither though goest..."

"How can we get Red to propose to Kate?"

"First I'm going to find out if it was Red out there tonight. He'll give himself away somehow, it if was. Whoever it was, chances are he'll want to blab about it to the other men." Logan's voice became harsh. "Sooner or later, I'll get him."

"Let's assume it wasn't Red. How do we get him together with Kate?"

He drew her up on top of him until her head was on his shoulder and began to stroke her hair. "I think that's where you come in. Remember that cowgirl outfit of yours, and the jamboree I talked about holding here? I figure you and Kate are about the same size. Are you following me, Liz'beth?"

She was not only following him, she was way ahead of him. "If I could just spend twenty minutes or so on Kate's face and hair she'd knock Red right off his feet. If it's glamour girls he likes, he's had one right under his nose all these years, but was just too blind to see it," Elizabeth said, excitement building in her voice. "She'll look smashing in that outfit; it's perfectly suited to her. And she's even slimmer than I am, so fit shouldn't be a problem."

"Do you think she'll let you at her? You and Kate haven't exactly been the best of friends."

Elizabeth grimaced. "Don't remind me. The only thing I'v
got going for me is that Kate doesn't know why I've alway
been so rude to her. Thank goodness, or I'd really feel like
fool."

"You were actually jealous over my brotherly affection to
ward Kate?" Logan asked with amusement.

"I didn't know it was brotherly, did I? I was jealous of an
woman who looked at you sideways—and you were alway
especially sweet to Kate."

"Well...she's a sweet girl. In fact, she probably deserve
better than Red," he said, with an edge to his voice now.

"Let's not jump to conclusions about that." She pause
"Even if it was Red, you couldn't really blame any man wit
eyes in his head for *looking*..." She allowed the thought t
trail off. "We really should have made sure the drapes wer
tightly closed."

"So now you're willing to exonerate him? Voyeurism is a
ugly business, Elizabeth, so I'd say it all depends on how lon
he spent outside that window."

There seemed nothing more she could add to that, bu
Elizabeth cautioned Logan once again about jumping t
conclusions. Still, every time Elizabeth remembered the loo
on Red's face when she and Logan had ridden in after th
storm, she experienced a sinking feeling deep within her.

An hour later, over breakfast, Elizabeth was still plannin
their strategy. "Since we can't hold the jamboree until yo
find out if Red is the guilty party, why don't we use the Ca
gary Stampede as an excuse to show off the 'new' Kate? Tha
way we really have nothing to lose. Since everyone dresse
to the nines in cowboy regalia, neither Kate nor Red will su
pect any ulterior motives. What do you think?"

"I think it sounds great, except for one thing. With you tw
dressed to kill we won't be able to keep our minds on wha
we're doing...We'll probably both lose. It's all I can do to ea
my breakfast with you sitting there." His gaze was sensual an

admiring. To Logan, Elizabeth looked particularly fresh and beautiful in her yellow sundress, hair swept up into a smooth little knot on top of her head.

"Logan, we must solve this problem," she admonished him softly though she understood his state of mind. Their morning's lovemaking had wrapped a golden net around them that would not easily admit the outside world.

"I know," he said with a sigh. "But you look so damned sweet that I'd rather nibble on you."

"Please, Logan, pay attention." A blush touched her cheeks.

"You've got it all."

"Then I trust I will have you to myself today? No bovines to rope? No broncos to bust?"

"And definitely no cooking duties for you," he added.

Her eyes flew to her watch. "Damn. I told Hank I would meet him at ten o'clock."

"Don't worry about it. I told him you wouldn't be there."

She frowned. "Why won't you understand? I like to cook."

He covered her hand with his. "Liz'beth...until I find out who it was last night I don't want you anywhere near the men. Will you promise to cooperate?"

She looked at him wordlessly, but immediate acknowledgment was in her eyes.

"I don't want anyone looking at you with wise eyes, I don't want your name bandied about. Because if that happened...I'd probably kill someone. And that isn't idle talk."

"I understand, Logan," she said quietly.

He leaned across the corner of the table and kissed her soundly. "I think we should mosey on down to the general store today, anyway, so you can start buttering up Kate."

Logan told her he needed an hour or two to make his rounds of the ranch, so Elizabeth took advantage of the time to place a phone call to Charles.

It was a difficult, depressing call, with continual interruptions from his secretary who seemed to be holding back a deluge of urgent calls. Charles was shouting in the background one minute, beseeching Elizabeth the next, and by the time she hung up the phone, her face was strained and streaked with tears. The knowledge that she had just said goodbye to an extremely dear friend—one whom she had just hurt badly—was difficult to accept. She decided to wait for Logan in her room, where she alternately cried and attempted to repair the damages. Realizing the futility of what she was doing, Elizabeth pulled herself together and moved outside onto the porch. A few minutes later Logan appeared, and she was able to summon a smile by the time he reached the steps.

"All set, buttercup?" he asked cheerfully.

Under his warm and admiring gaze Elizabeth forgot about everything else. She could only mirror his carefree happiness.

KATE'S GENERAL STORE did a steady business providing various commodities to all the ranch hands and cowboys within thirty miles of range country. Though the Opal L had its own supply house stocked with essentials, Elizabeth knew Logan's men frequently spent a good portion of their time and pay at Kate's store.

One reason for this became obvious as they entered the well-stocked interior and saw a cluster of men gathered around one of Kate's employees.

"That can't be Janet?" Elizabeth said, staring at the extremely well-endowed young woman. She remembered the daughter of Logan's chief horse handler and groom as a somewhat awkward teenager.

"Sure is. And as you can see business is booming. Every man here will probably spend twice as much as he planned just to impress her. Kate knew what she was doing when she hired her," Logan said dryly, his hand light on her back as he escorted her forward. "But you can bet she keeps a watchful eye on things, too."

"Logan!" Janet exclaimed, immediately breaking through her circle of admirers. "I just knew you'd get here one of these days!"

With eyebrows raised slightly, Elizabeth watched Logan being urged toward the coffeepot with lots of light, gay, flirtatious chatter.

Logan, lips twitching over Janet's well-rehearsed techniques, managed to reach around Janet and grab Elizabeth's hand. He pulled her gently to his side.

"I hope you brought lots of money with you," Janet was bubbling. "Because you should see the fancy new duds that just arrived. Kate ordered something special on account of the Stampede. You are going, aren't you, Logan?" She reached for a clean coffee mug.

"I'll be there," Logan said, holding up two fingers and nodding toward the coffee.

With a grudging glance at Elizabeth, Janet reached for another mug.

"Where's Kate?" Logan said.

"Oh, she's in the back going over dreary accounts," Janet replied as she filled both cups with strong-looking brew. "Why don't I go get her while you pick out your purchases?"

Elizabeth and Logan exchanged a look, which ended with a shrug of Elizabeth's slim shoulders and a valiant attempt not to laugh. "I guess I could use a few things," she said, needing to avoid Logan's smiling eyes.

Janet immediately became terribly interested in her. "Haven't I seen you someplace before? And yet I know you aren't from around these parts."

Elizabeth quickly mentioned her father and Sweetwater and past visits. She didn't want to open a discussion of her modeling career.

"I guess that explains it, then."

"Would you mind getting Kate now, Janet?" Logan put in, getting a little impatient with the chatter. "Elizabeth and I will look over the merchandise while you're gone."

Janet bounced off quickly then. All heads turned to watch as she crossed the floor.

"You weren't kidding about Kate knowing what she was doing, hiring Janet," Elizabeth commented in a laugh-choked whisper. "Dolly Parton, watch out."

"I understand Janet has a great head for business, too."

"Then she could easily take over this store if we can manage to get Kate to the altar."

"Shh, Kate's coming."

"Logan, what will I say to her?" Elizabeth asked, feeling suddenly nervous.

"You'll think of something—just be friendliness itself if inspiration doesn't strike."

"Logan!" Kate looked both surprised and pleased to see him. Elizabeth was afforded a curt nod. "What brings you out here?"

Kate, Elizabeth noticed, was dressed like a man in a plaid work shirt, Levi's and scuffed riding boots. It was little wonder that Red had been dragging his heels in spite of a very long courtship, if his attentiveness could be called that.

Nevertheless, a discerning eye could see that Kate had a lovely figure—slim and tall and shapely in all the right places. Her features, bereft of makeup, looked plain, and her skin was a little dried out from the western sun. Elizabeth had all the necessary remedies in her cosmetic case, and her fingers itched to work wonders on Kate. But how to put such a thing delicately? And was Red even worth going to such length for?

Elizabeth realized she was getting ahead of herself—for the moment she had to concentrate on winning Kate's friendship. When Kate and Logan had completed their greetings, she quickly interjected, "I need some more practical clothes while I'm visiting, so Logan was kind enough to bring me here. How are you, Kate?"

"Fine," Kate said, her eyes a little wary. "I...thought you weren't going to be staying long." Her voice was cool.

"I...well, I didn't want to miss the Calgary Stampede."

"Yes," Kate said. "It's the big topic of conversation these days."

"You know, of course, that Logan and Red are competing in some of the events," Elizabeth said hesitantly.

Kate looked at Logan in surprise. Then she frowned a little. "How do I get to know anything that's going on when you give Red so little time off, Logan?" She glanced back at Elizabeth with a slight flush on her face. "I rarely get to see him these days."

"He didn't happen to ride out here last night, then?" Logan questioned, his tone bland.

"Last night?" Kate looked confused. "No—wasn't he out on the range?"

"According to two of my men, he was. According to two others, he wasn't."

Elizabeth looked up in surprise. She had not known he'd been questioning his men.

Kate shook her head. "I haven't seen Red at all for the past week."

"It's his day off tomorrow," he assured her. "In fact, I'd like to have the two of you over for supper."

Kate looked at Elizabeth, as if judging the advisability of having Red in the same room with her.

"Come early," Elizabeth put in quickly. "I...I'd like to ask your advice on something."

"You would?" Kate eyed her skeptically. "I can't imagine what I could advise you on. But as it happens there is something I would like to ask you about, Elizabeth. And in my opinion there's no time like the present."

"Fine, Kate. What is it?"

Kate looked up at Logan. "Would you mind if Elizabeth and I went into the back room for a minute, Logan? This is...sort of personal."

Elizabeth and Logan looked at each other for an instant before Logan said, "By all means."

Following Kate's brisk lead, Elizabeth turned to shrug at Logan as she went.

In the cluttered back room, Kate said, "Look, this is bound to be an embarrassing subject for both of us and I won't even talk about it to Logan. I wouldn't be bringing it up at all if he hadn't asked those questions about Red—about where he was last night, I mean."

Elizabeth was frowning at her. "I don't follow, Kate. Are you saying Red was with you, after all?"

"No. But, Elizabeth, could you please tell me where Logan thinks Red was?"

Elizabeth began to shake her head slowly, but Kate was insistent. "Let me make it easy for you. Does Logan think that Red was around or near his house late last night?"

Elizabeth noticed that Kate's cheeks had begun to color a little. "And if he does?" she asked slowly.

Kate shook her head. "It wasn't Red, it was me."

Elizabeth stared at her.

"Listen...I told you this was going to be embarrassing."

"It was you...at the window?"

Kate managed a slight laugh, but it was obvious she was feeling terrible. "Yes, for a second or two. Well...maybe three. That's how long it took me to assure myself that it wasn't you and Red. When I saw clearly it was Logan I ran out of there fast, feeling like a fool and a snoop."

"But, Kate," Elizabeth said, trying to absorb this, "Why would you think I'd be in Logan's house with Red?"

"I had no way of knowing who was at home. And Red often sleeps at the house when Logan is out with the herd. They work shifts with each other, Elizabeth."

"So you naturally thought I'd leap at the chance to have an affair with Red?"

"Go ahead and laugh. But I happen to think Red is very good-looking—good-looking enough even for you. Add to that the fact that whenever you come out here he can't keep his eyes off you..."

"Okay, Kate, I get the picture. But surely after what you saw last night you do, too. Logan is the man I love. I've always loved him."

"Then why were you always so rude to me? It seemed logical to assume that it was on account of your feelings for Red."

Elizabeth took a deep breath. "No, Kate. It was because you and Logan seemed so fond of each other. Nobody thought to tell me that he was your half brother."

"I see," Kate said after a moment. "I figured Logan would have told you about all that in spite of my...sensitivity over it."

Elizabeth simply shook her head. "Not until two days ago."

"The big lug is very loyal, isn't he?" Kates eyes were suspiciously moist.

"I think he's just about perfect."

They smiled at each other.

"You, of course, think Red is perfect," Elizabeth said after a moment.

Kate dabbed at her eyes. "Gee...how could you tell?"

They both laughed.

After a moment of indecision, Kate said, "You know...Red and I have never actually slept together..."

"What does 'actually' mean?"

Kate laughed. "Well, all right. We haven't slept together, period."

"Kate..." Elizabeth said quietly. "How many years are you going to wait?"

"You think I'm a fool, don't you? Do you know what I'd give to have the same kind of relationship with Red that you and Logan share?" In a low voice, she ventured, "Last night in his study, Elizabeth? How did you...I mean, how could I...?"

"Do you really want to know?"

"Yes," Kate nodded. "Yes, I really do. I've been living out in the boonies too long, Elizabeth."

10

DAYS PASSED QUICKLY for Elizabeth and Logan, days full of laughter and happiness. Their relationship intensified and grew until both knew that regardless of what became of Kate and Red, they would find some way to stay together.

James continued to attend his meetings, and Elizabeth drove out to Sweetwater often, usually on the days when Logan was filling in for Red. And as for Red, he was spending more and more time with the blossoming Kate.

"HAS HE TAKEN THE TUMBLE YET?" Elizabeth asked as Kate admired herself front and rear in the mirror in Elizabeth's bedroom. The dazzling cowgirl outfit not only fitted beautifully, it was a perfect foil for Kate's Gypsy eyes and gleaming dark hair, which Elizabeth had drawn back into a sleek bun.

"No. . ." Kate answered slowly. "But only because I'm holding him at arm's length. I figure that after all the years I've waited for him to make his move, he deserves to pant a little while longer."

Elizabeth smiled and gave her a thumbs-up sign. "Kate, you look like a Spanish aristocrat getting ready for a day's outing. Talk about classy. If Red doesn't fall on his knees to you today, then he simply isn't worth the bother. Today you can have any man you want."

Kate looked pleased, but merely said, "Curse the luck—I'm a one-man woman." Then, hands on hips, she looked at

Elizabeth. "What about you? You always look good, of course, but aren't you going to get all dolled up, too?"

Elizabeth smiled and shook her head. "This is your day to shine, Kate."

Laughing, Kate came forward and kissed her on the cheek. Elizabeth felt quite choked up.

"You're awful cute sometimes, you know?" She placed her hands on her hips again and regarded Elizabeth with a smile. "You really think you look less than gorgeous in those blue jeans and that red undershirt? Honey...you look like a cross between Rita Hayworth and Doris Day."

Elizabeth laughed, but Kate had become serious. "You know, I was thinking about how Red and Logan both seem to admire classy-looking women. And do you know why?"

Elizabeth shook her head.

"Because they've spent so many years in the dust and the dirt and mud with their cattle that they're drawn to refined beauty like a thirsty man is drawn to water."

"Kate, that's very profound," Elizabeth mused, studying her new friend and potential sister-in-law.

Kate shrugged. "It just came to me in a blinding flash. That's why Logan doesn't want you to be his chief cook and bottle washer—he wants you to be the rainbow coloring his world."

Though she made light of Kate's insights, Elizabeth realized they held a lot of truth and explained why Logan tended to spoil and pamper her at every turn. Doing the very thing that he had spoken out on those many years ago. They frequently clashed over his attitude, and Elizabeth decided to prepare him a gourmet meal as a means of proving a point.

"Very fancy, sweetheart," he told her indulgently, thereby also proving a point.

"I suppose you prefer your everlasting beef and potatoes?" she demanded testily.

"You know what I prefer," he murmured, bringing her down onto his lap. "But if it pleases you to make these crepe things once in a while, that's okay, too."

Once she'd dealt with the 'crepe things,' she let him have it with both barrels, finishing her diatribe with, "I'm nothing but a sex object to you."

But by then his fingers had found the lace edge of her panties beneath her shorts, so she gave up. With a breathless sigh, she reasoned, "On the other hand, I could do worse, I suppose."

THE STAMPEDE had been under way for three days when they pulled into the exhibition grounds in two trailer-hauling vehicles. Logan's and Red's horses were in one trailer. The other provided overnight accommodation for humans.

They parked in their reserved spaces. Leading the horses through the throngs of people, they made their way to the stabling areas.

The mood was festive—hectic—and Elizabeth's eyes had never taken in such colorful Western regalia. Cowboys and Indians, both real and make-believe, crowded the walkways while squaredancers whirled in the streets to the tune of old-time fiddlers. The sound of thundering horses' hooves emanated from the racing stadium, mingled with the creak of harnesses and the clatter of passing chuck wagons. The smell of flapjacks being cooked at roadside hung in the air.

The foursome skirted the midway, passing a frontier casino and several livestock competitions finally making their way into a sawdust-strewn area where wranglers in rough demin clothes ministered to their best working horses.

Logan and Red each gave their mounts a careful going-over with hand and eye, making sure all was shipshape.

"What do you think about this Brahma bull thing?" Elizabeth asked Kate.

With an easy shrug, she replied, "Nothing either of them can't handle, but Red is going to win it. Now when it comes to the steer roping, Logan has a bit of an edge because of that fabulous horse of his. With the bronco busting," Kate went on with her predictions, "it'll probably be an even draw, because they are both the best there is. That is, when you cancel out the rodeo stars, who aren't real cowboys, anyway, and won't be competing in this event."

"If they're both so good at bronco riding, why would you automatically assume that Red can stay on a bull longer?" Elizabeth was thinking that surely anything Red could do, Logan could do better.

"Well, it's very simple," Kate said, tongue in cheek. "Red's got more of a bow in his legs 'cause of all the practicing he's done. Logan, on the other hand, has spent most of his time on the more practical aspects of ranching. Bulls generally don't need to be broken, Elizabeth."

Elizabeth sniffed. "Well, I guess I could have figured all that out for myself. Anyway, I still think Logan is going to win. I just hope nobody gets hurt."

"They won't," Kate replied. "Not until the chuck-wagon race. Then they're both going to get killed."

Elizabeth put her hand to her heart. "What are you saying?"

"Shh," Kate said, looking over her shoulder. "Logan told me not to tell you about it. But I think you should be prepared. It's hair-raising, Elizabeth, believe me. You see, it involves four chuck wagons, twenty riders and thirty-two horses, all making this mad dash for a single point on the track. There will be collisions, but for heaven's sake, don't scream, don't yell, don't faint. Don't do *anything* to break their concentration because, as you can imagine, it takes split-second timing to avoid an accident."

Before Elizabeth could voice any sort of breathless comment, Logan came up to her and wrapped his arm around her slim waist, drawing her against him. "Want to go look for James?" he queried, his eyes warm and loving looking on her upturned face. "I've got an hour or so before I have to put on my chaps."

Elizabeth had to bite her tongue to prevent herself from expressing her fright, anger and worry. It all seemed so foolhardy to her, and she could not really think about James at the moment.

"Well...if it isn't the Riverboat Gambler himself," Logan said, catching sight of James in the crowd. "Done up like you wouldn't believe, sweetheart. And there's a particularly lovely-looking woman hanging on his ruffled sleeve."

At this, Elizabeth followed Logan's gaze, "Mother!" she cried in astonishment. Breaking free of Logan she rushed over to the couple.

"Elizabeth! There she is, James!" Catherine exclaimed. She looked terrifically attractive in dark green slacks and a light mint blouse, with a caballero's hat to match.

Elizabeth hugged and kissed her mother and exclaimed over her in detail, sparing an admiring look or two at the dashing figure of James. "Well, just look at you two! And how come, Mother? I mean...aren't you a little early? James, why didn't you tell me Mother was coming?"

"What? And break up the love nest?" James said with a raised brow. "I'm lucky if I even get to see you."

"Yes, Elizabeth," Catherine said, "what's all this about you and John Logan? James tells me that the two of you will probably get married. I certainly hope so, because you seem to be breaking all the rules of propriety. What would your grandmother say?" At this, a brief smile, enhanced her mother's teasing expression.

"Mother," Elizabeth said patiently, "are you and she still at each other's throat?"

"Of course," Catherine said. "More now than ever before. You see, I had to tell her that I was flying out west early to

accompany James to one or two of his Gamblers Anony
mous meetings. Your grandmother did not take it grace
fully."

Elizabeth looked from her mother to her father. "The
James told you all about...his little mishap?"

"He did," Catherine said proudly. "Elizabeth, did yo
really think me so fragile? It was not your place to dash ou
here, you know. It was mine."

"I..." Elizabeth glanced at her father. "I was so afraid you'
be terribly hurt."

Catherine looked up at James, and their eyes immediatel
met. *Bonded* was the word that immediately came to mind

"Your father was worried, too. But I managed to put hi
mind at ease a bit." She turned back to Elizabeth. "How doe
it go, Elizabeth? For richer, for poorer...in sickness and i
health..."

For as long as you both shall live. Elizabeth finished si
lently, tears in her eyes as she looked at her father's face. Hi
expression was one of absolute adoration as he gazed down
at Catherine.

"Mother," Elizabeth said, brushing at her eyes, "I badl
want to introduce you to the second best man on earth."

She turned, and all her love welled up as Logan, taking hi
cue, came forward. "Mother—" she leaned in to him, the
reached up to touch his face "—this is the man *I* love."

"I MUST BE MAD TO LOVE YOU!" she told him hotly much later
when they had adjourned to their campsite to watch the fire
works.

"Listen, I came through it okay, didn't I? Won some priz
money, no broken arms, no broken legs—"

"Which still leaves that big hole in your head," Elizabet
broke in.

"Yeah," Red added, "don't you think you're getting a littl
old for all this, boss?"

"Shh," Kate said, "I think I heard a sore loser."

Red turned to look around before he caught himself. Laughing, he grabbed Kate. "I've got a winning kiss here for you, though," he said.

Elizabeth turned her attention back to Logan. "How is your head?" she asked, her fingertip delicately probing the bruised area around the cut on his forehead.

"It's fine," he said, catching her hand and brushing his lips against her knuckles.

"Cowboying is obsolete, Logan. When am I going to get that through your head?"

He smiled at her, and her heart did a little somersault. "Seeing as how I fell on it today, you just might be making some progress."

They were sitting on some logs they had positioned just beyond the spill of light from the camper. Kate had carefully laid out a blanket, for she was deathly afraid of soiling Elizabeth's outfit, despite the fact that Elizabeth had told her to keep it.

Out of the corner of her eye Elizabeth caught sight of the other couple's lingering embrace. "We seem to be making progress in other areas, as well," she whispered, directing Logan's attention with a brief nod toward Kate and Red.

"No doubt they're wishing they had the camper all to themselves. I know I am." He placed his arm around her shoulders.

Elizabeth leaned against him contentedly. "From the look of things, I'd say we've got the rest of our lives for that."

"A little hanky-panky doesn't necessarily mean a marriage proposal," Logan cautioned her in a low tone.

"Didn't you say something about having a dandy carrot for Red?"

Logan nodded. "I did, but I decided it would be better to let things happen naturally. My carrot amounted to a bribe, and Kate's too good for that."

"I agree. But tell me what it was."

"Half ownership in the ranch. It'll be a wedding gift now if he ever gets around to proposing."

Elizabeth pressed against him more tightly. "That's wonderful, Logan. You always did want Kate to share in the Opal L."

"That's right, and I think I'll play it safe and put it in Kate's name."

"Blood is thicker than water, they say. And, while I like Red, I have a feeling that constancy isn't his number-one character attribute."

"He's always come back to Kate, though."

"Fine. But a little insurance never hurt anybody."

The fireworks began then, hissing and crackling and booming, illuminating the black sky with shards of vivid color. Logan's arm remained firm and warm around her, and once or twice his lips brushed against her hair, making the night an entirely magical one for Elizabeth.

Sometime during the punctuation of brilliant lights, Red and Kate moved into the camper, and it was only then Logan's touch strayed as far as her breasts. "That little red shirt of yours has been driving me crazy all day. You delight me in a hundred thousand different ways, Liz'beth, even when you're trying so hard to be plain Jane."

The light brush of his fingers teased the nipples into hard little peaks that stood out against the thin material of her shirt, and then he brought his hands away to look at her with sensual satisfaction.

"That's it?" she asked, her voice attaining a now-familiar throbbing quality.

"There are still people milling around, sweetheart."

"We could kiss a lot," she said huskily, bringing her arms up to his shoulders and moistening her lips.

He looked at the offering. "You realize this is going to lead to an awful lot of frustration? And I have to bunk with Red tonight."

Her lips curved into a seductive smile. "Logan, I'm on fire here, and you're making jokes?"

"It's no joke. I tend to grope a lot in my sleep."

She pulled playfully at his ear. "I have noticed that about you, you know."

"Then you understand the problem."

"Listen, Logan, we're big boys and girls. And how much do you want to bet Kate and Red are bunking down together right this minute."

"I'm sure they are. But in a while they'll be coming out here all neat and tidy. Red will look pleased as punch and Kate's face will have that just-made-love-to look on it, and then they'll both behave themselves for the rest of the night."

"If Kate were smart, she'd hold out for that marriage proposal."

"The way you did?" he teased.

"What you've just done here Logan is remind me that you've never actually proposed to me. Oh, sure, sure," she went on when he was about to speak. "You talk about us flitting around the world together—when you know perfectly well I detest flying. But you've never actually said, 'Will you marry me,' have you?"

"Will you?"

"Yes."

"Good. Now give me that kiss you've been promising."

"I thought you didn't want to get frustrated?"

"I've changed my mind," he growled softly as his hands slowly began to massage her back, causing her thin knit shirt to brush against her nipples.

Her hand moved up behind his head, and she buried her fingers in the softness of his hair as she pulled his head down. Her lips brushed against his with a slow, teasing fire; her

tongue traced the sensual curve. She brought her other hand
to his cheek, stroking the rough growth of day-old whiskers
as she tugged and toyed with his lips, flirting with the fire she
was building in him.

Logan's gentle massage now included the curves of her
breasts. But still he did not take charge of the kiss, letting her
set the pace. He caught at her mouth in equal response only
meeting the darting blade of her tongue, but not bypassing
it with the force of his rising desire. That is, until her mouth
opened fully on his, her lips and hands exerting pressure as
she moaned softly in frustration.

He met her plea deeply then. Her waist, her rib cage, her
shoulder blades, all felt the drawing pressure of his hands and
fingers as the passion of their kiss grew to unbearable heights.

Finally they drew apart, panting with need. Logan spoke
raggedly. "I knew this was going to happen. Why did I let you
tempt me?"

"It serves you right for having such a sexy mouth," she returned breathlessly in her defence. "And for...fondling me
like that."

"Like what?" he asked, his voice thick, while his hand
continued to stroke her back.

"You know very well you were getting me aroused."

"Did I? Tell me more, Liz'beth."

"I think we'd better stop this, don't you?" She shifted a little so she was halfway off his lap. Her hand accidentally
touched the hard swell beneath the fly of his jeans, and he let
out a tortured groan.

"What are you trying to do to me?" he demanded hoarsely.

"I'm sorry, darling," she soothed, facing forward to re-
sume watching the fireworks. "I promise I won't touch you
again."

"Wonderful," Logan drawled. "Tease me, torture me, call
me darling—and then promise not to touch me again. I'm

keeping score, you know, Liz'beth, and sooner or later I'm going to be collecting."

"Sooner, I hope," she said fervently, very aware of the throbbing inside of her.

"Whose stupid idea was it for us to spend the night here, anyway?" he complained.

"Yours, darling. You thought you'd be too tired for the long drive home. Red thought so, too."

"What is this? A man reaches the tender age of thirty-nine and everyone starts ganging up on him?"

"Sweetheart, I meant that Red thought he'd be too tired, as well."

"Oh."

After a calming period had passed, Elizabeth gingerly took his hand and asked, "How did you like my mother, Logan? Don't you think she's a dear?"

"Yes, Liz'beth. She's lively and sweet. And James is a very happy man." He removed his hand from her grasp to place his arm around her shoulders.

Elizabeth sighed happily. "He managed to come up with a winning hand, after all."

Logan smiled. "I guess you could say it was in the cards."

"For us, too," she said, snuggling against him. "Because if it weren't for that disastrous poker game, you and I would never have got together again."

"Do you want to bet?" he said, looking down at her, his eyes both tender and teasing.

"I don't know. What would the odds have been?"

"Ten to one in my favor. I didn't want to go through life without you. I would have found a way."

She closed her eyes as she leaned against him, seeing her own fireworks display beneath her lids. Love and ecstasy radiated and pulsed with a sexual energy that would forever after hold her in its thrall.

"Logan," Elizabeth said softly. "You were so very right, yo know."

"About what, sweetheart?"

"About the fact that neither of us should entirely give u what we are for the other. We have so very much to give t each other, such an interesting blend to create. But we ca only do that really well if we each hold firm to our ident ties—to who and what we are. If things don't work out b tween Red and Kate, it won't really matter—we can live wit temporary separations. And then…oh, darling, the antic pation—the things we'll have stored up to share. You and will set the sky on fire when we come together. We'll crea fireworks far and beyond what we're looking at now, to mak up for every single day that we're apart."

"You make it almost sound bearable, high-fashion model he murmured.

"It will be, cowboy. I think if we can make it through th first twenty-four hours, we just might stand a chance o making it for a whole week."

"And then what, sugar lips?" he teased her warmly.

"Well, then naturally I would expect you to fly out wee ends."

"Weekends. Every weekend."

"Yes. And then I could fly out here every summer."

"And what about Christmas?"

"I think it would be nice if we took turns on that, and th long-distance calls, as well."

"Long-distance calls."

"Yes. Every night."

They looked at each other—a somber, intense look that le no room for teasing.

"And mornings, too, if you could manage it," Elizabet said past a lump in her throat.

His other arm moved around her as he bent to kiss a single tear from her lashes, and then in a deep, whisper-soft voice, he said, "Good try, my sweet love...but I would prefer to move heaven and earth..."

Epilogue

"HOW DO I LOOK?" Logan said, straightening his tie and adjusting the lapels of his dove-gray dinner jacket.

Elizabeth made a thorough visual inspection, for they were dressing for one of her grandmother's infamous formal dinner parties.

"You look wonderful, Logan—except for one thing."

"What's that?" He looked down at his ruffled shirt and dusted off a flick of lint from his 'dress' denims.

"That was it—you just caught it," she said, her eyes dancing.

His eyes laughed back at her. "Minx. You could at least look a little horrified."

She shook her head as her eyes moved over him again. "Logan, you could start a whole new trend. Look at it this way, darling, it's the perfect cultural blend between east and west."

Logan nodded as he admired himself in the full-length bedroom mirror. "And you thought that particular twain wasn't ever going to meet," he said with satisfaction.

"Well, you tricked me, darling. I was expecting a clash of sorts."

His smile flashed, and he pulled her against him, his mouth suddenly warm and demanding on hers.

"Don't you ever get enough?" she breathed when he left her lips to seek out the pulse that beat at the base of her perfumed throat.

"Of you, Liz'beth? You need to ask?"

"But we'll be late, Logan," she protested. "And Grandmother so admires punctuality."

"She thinks I'm an author so she'll forgive me anything."

"You are an author, Logan," she reminded him.

"One lucky stab at fiction." He backed her up against the bed.

The Dying Breed was no work of fiction. A work of art, perhaps..."

"I made it all up," he insisted. "You still see *me* going strong, don't you?" He rubbed his hardness against her, nearly prompting a backward fall to the bed for Elizabeth. She held on grimly.

"Absolutely no, Logan. I've spent the last half hour getting ready. James and Mother will probably be arriving there soon, and we did promise him moral support."

Reluctantly Logan released her.

Elizabeth struggled to control her own longing. "This is the first time they've come back for a visit, and I'd like it to go as well as possible."

"It's my wish for them, too," Logan agreed, stroking her cheek.

"This sounds corny as hell...but have I told you lately that I love you?"

"Over the past year or so, you mean? In between rounds of TV studios and casting directors and dancing lessons and—"

"Has it been terrible for you?" she broke in.

"I got a best-seller out of it, didn't I?" he replied. "And a good dose of the ranch now and again, too." He kissed her lips softly, careful not to disturb their glossy perfection. "Kate and Red are well settled in and making good profits all around, while I..." He stopped for a moment, then went on, "While I find myself adapting to this side of the trail a whole lot better than I thought I would. You might even say I've been enjoying myself a lot. I'm even getting to like that grand-mother of yours. But don't tell James, okay?"

"You got my word, partner," Elizabeth said, her eyes moist. "Logan, promise me something? Promise me that if ever you feel it's just getting a little out of hand for you, you'll tell me? Don't ever sacrifice your happiness for me. You are abso-lutely the most important thing in the world to me, and I just couldn't bear it if—"

He placed a finger against her lips to stop the worried flow of words. Next came his lips, warm and enveloping and un-caring of the damage they evoked. Then his breath was warm in her ear as he murmured intensely, "Liz'beth, *you* are my happiness."

COMING NEXT MONTH

#89 THE WINGS OF MORNING
Jackie Weger

There was something about cocksure
Garrett Stark that really got under
Rachel Cameron's skin. And the feeling was
mutual. As County Sheriff, Garrett was tempted
to arrest her for disturbing his peace....

#90 LISTEN WITH YOUR HEART
Jane Edwards

Though Nicholas blamed himself for Casi's
blindness, Casi knew it had been an accident. His
stimulation of her other senses, however, was
definitely deliberate.

#91 TRUE COLORS Jayne Ann Krentz

Seeking out the man who'd once loved you, then
betrayed you, was no easy task. But Jamie
needed answers to the question burning in
her heart.

#92 AN IMPRACTICAL PASSION
Vicki Lewis Thompson

Mother Nature was hitting Sydney hard—how
could she contend with both a hurricane *and*
wild and sexy Colin Lassiter? Yet the last thing
she wanted to do was run for cover....

WORLDWIDE LIBRARY IS YOUR TICKET TO ROMANCE, ADVENTURE AND EXCITEMENT

Experience it all in these big, bold Bestsellers— Yours exclusively from WORLDWIDE LIBRARY WHILE QUANTITIES LAST

To receive these Bestsellers, complete the order form, detach and send together with your check or money order (include 75¢ postage and handling), payable to WORLDWIDE LIBRARY, to:

In the U.S.
WORLDWIDE LIBRARY
P.O. Box 1397
Buffalo, NY
14240-1397

In Canada
WORLDWIDE LIBRARY
P.O. Box 2800, 5170 Yonge Street
Postal Station A, Willowdale, Ontario
M2N 6J3

Quant.	Title	Price
_____	**WILD CONCERTO**, Anne Mather	$2.95
_____	**A VIOLATION**, Charlotte Lamb	$3.50
_____	**SECRETS**, Sheila Holland	$3.50
_____	**SWEET MEMORIES**, LaVyrle Spencer	$3.50
_____	**FLORA**, Anne Weale	$3.50
_____	**SUMMER'S AWAKENING**, Anne Weale	$3.50
_____	**FINGER PRINTS**, Barbara Delinsky	$3.50
_____	**DREAMWEAVER**, Felicia Gallant/Rebecca Flanders	$3.50
_____	**EYE OF THE STORM**, Maura Seger	$3.50
_____	**HIDDEN IN THE FLAME**, Anne Mather	$3.50
_____	**ECHO OF THUNDER**, Maura Seger	$3.95
_____	**DREAM OF DARKNESS**, Jocelyn Haley	$3.95

	YOUR ORDER TOTAL	$_____
	New York residents add appropriate sales tax	$_____
	Postage and Handling	$ .75
	I enclose	$_____

NAME _____

ADDRESS _____ APT.# _____

CITY _____

STATE/PROV. _____ ZIP/POSTAL CODE _____

WW3R

Take 4 best-selling love stories FREE

Plus get a FREE surprise gift!

What the press says about Harlequin romance fiction...

"When it comes to romantic novels...
Harlequin is the indisputable king."
— *New York Times*

"...always with an upbeat, happy ending."
— *San Francisco Chronicle*

"Women have come to trust these
stories about contemporary people,
set in exciting foreign places."
— *Best Sellers*, New York

"The most popular reading matter of
American women today."
— *Detroit News*

"...a work of art."
— *Globe & Mail*, Toronto